Robbery & Betrayal

Written by:
Anthony Gardner

Cadmus Publishing
www.cadmuspublishing.com

ACKNOWLEDGMENTS

Sugamom, I know you're smiling down on me, love you granny! First and foremost, I would like to thank God, because without him none of this would have happened. I would like to thank the strongest woman that I know, which is my mom. Thanks for loving me and putting up with my crazy ass. Shout out to all my sisters; Missy, you mean the world to me! Nisha, Netta, and Auntie Tanya, Dizzy love y'all. Vontray, you already know what it is bro. Thanks for always sending that money, you better promote me. Cardale, love you lil bro! Shout out to the dirt, especially my cutthroats, crafty, and can't forget the flowers. You already know what it is. Dirt gang or don't bang! This has all been a hell of a journey, but I made it. Nothing could stop me. I'm going all the way up!

Shout out to all my federal penitentiary men and all the men locked up in the state. Too many names to name, but ya know I mess with y'all the long way. I'm Trending! Believe that.

Most of all shout out to all the haters and gossipers. Thanks for always gossiping and keeping me relevant. Without y'all gossiping and hating I wouldn't be able to promote my brand. I also want to shout out all the friends and females that turned their back on me. Honestly, thanks because without y'all leaving me for dead how would I have made room for the new friends and females in my life? Most of all, I thank all my nieces and nephews for not forgetting about their uncle. Do something in life period.

Free all the real ones. Crypto, love you bro. Crafty Tiketh thanks for staying solid. From KMP to OHC. Harlem Finest poke3, Shane Tay-Tay L Mace5-1, Luke3, ccrazy3, T. Mel Marstone's J stones, Peewee 3.4.5 Killa Brim1.2.3, Frog 1.2.3, Sponge 1.4.6. Antwone love you cuzzo, Baby kit, Baby Tray, C-Rocc3, Brodie 1.2.3, Crypto 3.4., Blue Devil 4, CTE, Mel-Mel, pill C-, keith 3.4. Crazy Dee 1.2.3.4, Milly 4, Maxwell, D-mac, Hen, Slice, Capone, Boocoo, Jaccie Boy 2.3.4, Tiny E, Lil E, Ric Roc 5. Big Watt, Baby Watt, Bird snake Dee, Tiki, Shadyboy, Headache 1.2, Peaches, China 1,2, Jaccie girl, T-Hottie, Mrs. Keith, Keda Roc 1.2.3 Den 1-5. I don't have room for everyone, so cuzz don't be mad I ran out of room for your name, but y'all know it's Bulletproof love you know I never can forget about you sis the one and only Curtisha AKA Shay. 39Ts, DPC Ave. NeNe and, Keke I love you baby girls. Pokey love you BF, drink one for me lol. Ice man 4, C Ragg 4, Poke4, RIP C-dog, Crazy-O Big D.

Nephew Lil Vontray, stay focused. Don't let me come home and beat your ass lol. All my nieces, y'all already know, no boyfriends until y'all 30yrs old lol. Love y'all! Uncle Ronnie damn, it'll be good to hear from you.

Want to give a special shout out to all the good men in the F.B.O.P. that knows how to stand tall, and to the ones that haven't, don't buy my book or read it. Oil and water don't mix period! Snow, Puncho, Khead, Kiko, Firt, Smiley, Termite, Chop, T-Roc, DRiu, Tone, Tough, Mumbles, Fats, Smash, Wayne, Lips, Moody, Kento, Kipnap, Creed, BG, YA, Don Juan, DLoc, Hardroc, Ducc, Sinbad, Gride, Schoolboy, Tru, Izzy, Ice, Timebomb, GB, Skibo, Red, Soup, Jay, Stilt, Rambo, Mikeloc, Rara, Tee, Play, Mardy, Montey, and, Professor. Too many too name so blame I don't have enough room and not my heart.

Special shout out to all the women that come and gone out of my life, know I appreciated the phone calls, visits, text and, pictures. Y'all kept me sane over the years even if you do come and, go lol. This too much for anybody I understand that period!! Chicc,

Sunni, Sheneak, Asia, Melody, Shanae. No hard feelings Mo-Mo, Feleica, Kim, Tameka, Ricca, Darnetta, Codey, Tam, Lil Momma (syc). Blue, Kelly, Sheray, Special TIGI, Leslie, and you already know you'll forever hold a special place in my heart. Q-Abner you and the girls.

Loyalty Over, Royalty!! I'm Trending!! TRU QUEEN TASHA MCGORDON thanks for everything my love.

CONTENTS

CHAPTER ONE

Can I get a pack of Newport's and a pint of Gin, please?

"You need to tell your mother to get off that sofa and stop sending you up here to get her smokes," the Korean Clerk said as she rung up the Newport's and bottle of Gin for Brandy.

Brandy was fifteen years old, but the Koreans knew her mom, so they broke the law, and when you live in South Central LA, anything goes.

"I tell her that every time she sends me down here, but it goes in one ear and out the other," Brandy replied.

As she headed out the store and began to walk to her house, her mind began to wonder. She always dreamed of saving enough money and leaving the hood, and she was tired of hearing gunshots and helicopters. When she was getting deep into thought, gun shots went off. She was distracted for five seconds and went right back to daydreaming. Hearing gunshots in L.A. was expected, but Brandy was tired of it.

Brandy's daydreaming was interrupted once again when she saw Clappa and Black walking in her direction. Clappa, Black, and Brandy all went to the same school, and she would let them cheat off her work whenever they did come to class, but it wasn't a problem because she thought Clappa was cute, and being that Black was his right-hand man, she would let him cheat too.

"Take this bag and keep walking."

Before she could reply, Clappa shoved a black Jan sports bookbag in her hand and kept walking. She wasn't sure if she should drop the bag or do as she was told. By the time she made up her mind, it was too late. She saw flashing lights and heard tires screeching as the gang task force appeared from every corner. Her mind told her to keep walking, but that little crush she had on Clappa made her look back to see if he was ok. The sight of Clappa and Black on their knees with guns drawn on them made her wonder what kind of trouble they got themselves into and what was in this book bag she was holding.

Later that night, Brandy was in her room. She'd been staring at the bookbag for the past hour, trying to decide if she should look in it or not. A knock at the front door startled Brandy. She quickly jumped up to look out the window. She began praying, hoping that it was one of her mother's male friends and not the police. When she looked out the window, she didn't see any familiar cars or squad cars, so she blew it off and laid it down.

"Brandy, get ya ass down here!"

Brandy's heart began to race, and her mind quickly went back to the bookbag. She panicked as she tried to find a place to hide it. Then she tossed it in the back of her closet and put some clothes on the top cover it up then rush downstairs.

"What's wrong Ma?"

When she approached the front door, she saw Clappa standing there with a grin on his face and her mom sticking something in her robe pocket while she headed back to her bedroom.

What the fuck, my mom is letting me have a boy over this late? I must be dreaming! she thought.

"Brandy. Brandy. Brandy," Clappa said as he waved his hand in her face to take her out of her thoughts. "Where's my bag?

"Nigga don't ever put me in the middle of ya shit! Don't ever hand me no bag and tell me to keep walking. Then you pop up at nine-o-clock on a fucking school night talking about where's my bag. Nigga fuck you!"

As Brandy went on and on, Clappa couldn't help but smile and lick his lips. Seeing her going off was turning him on, and she didn't know it. Brandy stood 5'4, weighed a hundred and thirty pounds, with curves only a drag race driver could drive. Her bow-legged walk would turn any guy on, not to mention she had a camel toe out of this world that she kept on display. To top everything off, she was a redbone with a perfect set of lips.

"Nigga you think…"

"Man, you talking too much. Go get the bag. As a matter of fact, come on!" Clappa interrupted her, grabbed her by the arm, and marched her upstairs. "I need my shit; we can do all the talking you want after I get my bag."

When they entered Brandy's room, Clappa was in shock by how nice it was.

Damn, this chick got a fish tank and a big screen T.V? I know her piece of shit mother didn't buy it. I just had to give her $40.00 to speak to her. Fuck it, she probably likes all these other hoes out here fucking and sucking on the low! Clapper's thoughts were running wild.

"Where is the bag?"

"Damn nigga, relax! I had to stash it, and I didn't know what you and Black crazy ass had going on." When Brandy handed Clappa the bag, he quickly unzips it, making sure his 45, 9mm, and money was still there. When he dumped everything on the bed, Brandy's eyes grew wide.

"What's wrong?" "I never saw that much money or guns in my life" "Damn; Maybe I misjudged you, Lil Momma. Here take this!

"What's that?" "Five- hunnit "I don't need or want your money" "What, bitch you too "good for. "

Before Clappa Could get another word out, Brandy cocked back and slapped him with all her might Clappa quickly grabbed her and tried to restrain her as she punched, slapped, and scratched him.

"What the fuck!"

"Ain't no nigga ever call me a bitch, and I'll be damn if I start letting you call me one today!! Brandy replied with tears running down her face. "I did ya ass a favor by holding ya bag and letting you in my house, so you betta talk to me like you got some fucking sense!"

"You're right, Lil Mamma. I'm one hunnit percent wrong for that, and I apologize. Please take the Money as a gift; it would make me feel better." Clappa tried cheering Brandy up, but her feelings were already hurt. She did him a favor not because of the money, and she did it out of the kindness of her heart because she has a crush on him.

The next day Black and Clappa met up to split the money. Clappa had to tell Black about the five hundred he gave Brandy the night before because he didn't want him to think some funny shit was going on. He wasn't sure how he would feel about the whole situation because

Black wasn't pressed for giving a female anything besides a mouth full of dick.

"Damn, homie, so you tricking now?" Black asked jokingly

"Nah, Cuzz, it ain't even like that." It's simply a favor for a favor; that's all.

Well, I hope so. You have been getting real soft on me lately, cuzz".

"Soft doesn't run through my blood Cuzz, replied Clappa defending himself.

"So, let's talk about the other night when you let them old niggas reach for the strap at the Gambling Shack?"

"Damn Cuzz, so that's how you gonna ride me? I slipped up for a second, but you saw once I popped those two shots. In the air, his old ass saw shit was real!" "Exactly, homie, the same two shots you let off is what caused the hood to call the police; you need to tighten up cuzz.

"But we got away, I slid the bag to Lil Mamma, and the only thing they could arrest us for was resisting arrest, which I don't understand because we complied with them crackers."

"We going count the rest of this after school. I gotta meet up with some people."

"Yea, I need to see Brandy."

"Damn, Cuzz, she got you open like that; did you even hit?" "It ain't even like that."

The ride to school was awkward for Clappa and Black; the two sat in silence as they let the L.A. morning breeze flow through the car. Clappa had one thing on his mind, and that was Brandy. I couldn't wait until his fourth-period class came around because that's when he would see her. The day seemed like it was dragging as he anxiously waited for the bell the ring and ended the third period. I rushed out of the class and headed to Mrs. Gold's class once the bell finally rang. I took a seat in the front row because that's where Brandy always sat.

"Damn homie, what's going on with you?" Black asked as he headed towards the back of the class, where he and Clappa usually sat.

"Chill, Cuzz, I'm tryna handle something."

"Since when do you sit in the front?" asked Brandy as she took the only seat left, which was next to Clappa.

"I need to see ya homework!"

"I didn't do it because you had me up late last night, and I went to sleep once you left."

"Damn, baby, I feel bad; let me take you out."

"Hell No! I'm not some ho you think you can just fuck!"

"Damn, why you gotta be so loud? You got the whole class laughing, even Mrs. Gold's old ass!"

For the rest of the fourth period, Clappa sat in silence. To make things worse, every time he looked back at Black; he gave him that I-told-you-so look. When the bell rang, Brandy slid Clappa a note.

Clappa, I'm sorry for putting you on blast in front of the whole class earlier. I'm still a lil mad about last night. The way you called me a bitch was outta line. If you want to go out, pick me up at 8 pm tonight and don't be late. Or I might change my mind.

P.S. Don't think for one second that you're getting any pussy, because I'm a virgin.

"A Virgin?" Clappa said aloud, then looked around to see if anybody heard him. *I'm shocked nobody hit that yet; now I really have to hit,* he thought.

"What's good, Cuzz, we still on for the night?" Black asked, bringing Clappa back to reality.

"Nah, cuzz, I got a date!"

Black walked off, shaking his head. Clappa rushed to the Beverly Center Mall and went to men's land, where he purchased a bottle of Jimmy Choo Cologne for men and the Fendi jacket, shoes, and pants.

I know this shit not real with these cheap ass prices. He thought.

When he was done shopping, he rushed home to take a shower and try on the new outfit he just bought. He rolled a blunt, and then seven-thirty came rolling around. He jumped in his 2004 two-door Yukon on 24's, which no one at school knows he has. Clappa was always paranoid that somebody would tell on him. After Black's older brother was told on by his uncle, he looked at everybody as a potential snitch.

Clappa's palms began to sweat as he got closer to Brandy's house. He tried to calm his nerves with a nice blunt, but taking Brandy's virginity had him anxious. When he arrived in front of her house, he checked himself in the mirror to make sure everything was on point. He tucked his 9mm under his Fendi Shirt and headed to the front door. Brandy answered the door in a robe, and Clappa immediately thought he was about to hit it.

"Why aren't you dressed?"

"I am dressed," she said before dropping her robe to reveal a skin-tight Gucci dress with the matching blouse and some red bottoms to match

That shit has to be fake; she can't afford that kind of shit, Clappa thought.

"You got ya license?" She asked as they headed back to Clappa's truck.

"Yeah."

When they got in the truck, Clappa stashed his 9mm in the stash box. The two went to "Chinx," a soul food restaurant that had everybody going crazy. They had a good time and enjoyed each other's company. They laughed, joked, and got to know each other really well.

"How do you get all that money, Clappa?"

"How do you think?"

"I hope you not out there hurting people."

"Listen, baby, I do what I have to do to survive. It's a dog-eat-dog world, and sometimes these dogs bite, and I have to bite back."

"That doesn't sound too good, Clappa."

"What about you, how you make your money? I saw the big screen T.V, and expensive fish tank in ya room."

"You saw my fish? I love my fish; they keep me company when I'm lonely, and the sound of their water filter drowns out the sounds of gunshots all night. To answer your question, I work at Macy's."

"Thank god," Clappa replied.

"For what?"

"I thought you were into some other shit!!"

"Like what?"

"Nothing. I'm just happy that you work!"

"Thanks, but it's hard to save money because my mom charges me $500 a month for rent."

"Don't worry, Lil Mamma, if you ride with me, you won't have to worry about money ever again."

"Yeah, ok, we will see."

CHAPTER TWO

After Clappa's and Brandy's first date, they were inseparable, and they did everything together. Black started to feel the same type of way as he watched his partner in crime slowly pull back from him. Clappa had saved forty-thousand from all the prior robberies they did together, so he was enjoying his time with his new girl. He still never hit, but he was patient because he had genuine feelings for her.

It was their two-month anniversary, and he wanted to surprise Brandy with a promise ring, but she was nowhere to be found. He tried calling her phone, but she never answered, so he left voice mail after voice mail. When she didn't show up for the fourth period, that's when he knew something was really wrong because Brandy never missed school. He drove to her job, and her co-workers said that she hadn't been to work all day. He rushed to her house. He burst through the door and ran straight upstairs to find her laid on her bed, hugged up with her pillows crying her eyes out.

"Damn baby, I been looking for you everywhere. Why haven't you picked up your phone? Is everything ok?"

"My manager called me to work today to tell me I was fired because they have me on camera stealing!"

"Huh? That doesn't even sound like you," replied Clappa."

"I swear, baby, I never stole a day in my life. I earned everything I own."

"Damn baby, I'm sorry to hear that. Don't worry, I will take care of you!"

"And to top everything off, when I tell my mom about it, the bitch gone tell me I need to find another way to make money because she still wants her five-hunnit every month. I swear I hate her!"

"Don't cry, baby. I will pay the rent. That's not a big deal. But since ya mother on bullshit, you need to let her know that I'm moving in, so make room.

"Moving in? Nigga are you crazy? My mamma is not going to let that happen."

"Well let's see, she just pulled in, so let's find out!" Clappa said as he looked out the window.

"Where are you going to sleep?"

"In the bed with you!"

"That's not happening! I never had a boy."

"Well, as I said, make room!"

Brandy and Clappa headed downstairs to speak to Brandy's mom. Brandy couldn't believe she was about to step into her man in such away. She never thought she would be asking if a boy can move in. Nervousness took over her body as she began to approach her mother. Clappa played the background because, in all reality, he was also nervous.

"Mom? Well, you know I got fired today?"

"Yeah, so what that mean?" She said in a nasty tone.

"Um. Ummm. Um."

"Girl, spit it out. I don't have all day. My shows are about to come on, and you're wasting my time right now!"

"Well, Clappa felt terrible for me and said he would pay the $500 every month if he can move in."

"You must be out ya god damn mind if you think I'm going let one of these no-good gang-banging lil niggas live in my house! I know ya fast ass better slow down. I'm not trying to raise no damn grandkids. I didn't raise no ho, lord knows I did enough hoing for the both of us.

"I never been with Clappa. I'm still a virgin."

"Virgin my ass! Ain't no man is going to pay a woman rent and not get something out of it. You sucked his dick or something."

"Listen moms," Clappa interrupted. "I never fucked your daughter, got my dick sucked, or even tongue kissed the girl. Maybe I want to take her out of a fucked-up situation. Either way, here is fifteen-hunnit for the next three months, take it or leave it. But if you take this money, I come with it. If you don't take it, I will move ya daughter out today. What's it going be?"

The room got quiet while everybody soaked up what Clappa just said. He didn't even know where he grew the courage to stand up to her like that.

"First of all, you lil young disrespectful nigga, fifteen-hunnit ain't shit. I will wipe my ass with that, but I'm going to take it. These are my fucking rules while ya young asses are laid up in my house. No loud music, no missing school, no company, and when I have my company, you stay ya asses in that room. Last but not least, I don't want to hear you fucking, and I don't want to smell sex! Are we clear?"

"Yeah," they both said at the same time, trying to hide their excitement.

"Oh yeah, be in the house by nine or don't come in the place at all. Since you got so much money, Mr. Baller, I want half on every bill in this mufucka, and that's including food."

"Dang, mama, that's a lot! What about all those dudes that sleep over? Do they ever pay anything?" asked

Brandy.

"Of course, honey, nothing around here is free. Remember that!"

"Ok, well, here is another grand for the bills," Clappa said, peeling off ten crispy hundred-dollar bills.

Brandy's mom snatched the money and went straight to her bedroom. Brandy and Clappa smiled at each other, knowing they just pulled off the impossible. Clappa knew her mom would play hard, but one thing he learned in the streets is that money talks and bullshit walks. The two of them jumped in Clappa's Yukon and headed towards downtown LA. Brandy began to look confused when he pulled in front of the Harlem Western Inn, and she knew that the hotel was known for two things, and that were drugs and hoe's

"Why are we here?"

"Black and I live here, and I'm coming to get my stuff!"

"Ok, good," Brandy replied in relief, knowing that he wasn't expecting to get any pussy!"

"I've been staying here with Black for some time now. We pay $750 a month."

They jumped out of the truck and headed towards the elevator. Brandy realized that she misjudged Clappa. She thought he was like the rest of the boys and just wanted to have sex with her, but she was starting to realize that he was different. Brandy was so caught up in her thoughts that she didn't even realize the elevator came to a stop.

"Are you going to sit there, or are you coming?" Clappa asked

"Oh, sorry"

When they arrived in front of room 39, they could smell weed seeping through the door and Nipsey Hussle blaring through the speakers. Clappa looked back and gave Brandy a slight grin hoping she wasn't getting uncomfortable. He slowly put the key in the keyhole. When Clappa opened the door, Brandy got the shock of her life. China and Chiquita from their fourth-period class were on their knees, sharing Black's dick. They were sucking like it was the last piece of dick on earth. Brandy's stomach turned because she never thought girls in her class got down like that. Black continued to puff his blunt while China deep throated him, bringing him to a climax. Black stood up so he could dump his load in China's mouth.

"Make sure you share some of that nut with Chiquita," Black commanded.

"Oh Shit, what's up Cuzz?" he said to Clappa when he finally realized he was standing there.

Brandy was trying to hold back the vomit building up in her mouth. Black walked over to Clappa butt-naked and tried to hand him a blunt, but Clappa denied it. Clappa was embarrassed that Brandy had to witness this and wondered how she would look at him now.

"Hi Clappa, Hi Brandy," China and Chiquita said at the same time.

"Don't ya see my girl standing here? Put some clothes on!"

"Stop acting like you never saw me naked before," China shot back.

Clappa ignored her and rushed to the bedroom to start packing his things. China kept replaying in Brandy's head, and the thought of Clappa seeing China naked was making her mad. Brandy stood there with her arms folded, waiting for an explanation.

"What's up, Cuzz?" Black asked.

"I'm moving out, and I'm moving in with my girl. She got fired and needs my help."

"Damn, Cuzz, I wish you woulda been told me this. I woulda made other plans, but I respect it".

Brandy was shocked by how many guns Clappa keeps pulling out from the closet. She wanted to help him pack but hearing what China said got her in her feelings. Now she was second-guessing if she wanted Clappa to move in.

"Did you hear that, Chiquita? With Clappa moving in with his bitch we can't have any more orgies."

Brandy ran out of the room, and without saying any words, she began to beat on China. Clappa, and Black rushed to China's rescue by pulling Brandy off of her, but her rage and anger kept her going. She scanned the room when they finally got her off China, and she spotted a chrome .357 magnum on the dresser. She rushed for the gun and pointed it at China and Chiquita.

"Get naked bitches, since ya on Clappa's dick so much take all his shit to the truck ass naked!"

"Relax, Brandy, it's not even like that," Chiquita pleaded.

"Bitch, it is like that! Now hurry ya hoe ass up and fill that fucking truck."

Anger was in Brandy's eyes as she watched China and Chiquita fill Clappa's truck. Clappa and Black stood back laughing while they shared a blunt. The conversation between Clappa and Black got a little emotional when Black told him that he was all he had. It made Clappa feel like he was turning his back on his boy, and that wasn't the case. Clappa just wanted to do what was best for his girl.

When Clappa and Brandy got to the house, they immediately started unloading the truck. Clappa had so much stuff that Brandy had to rearrange her closet and bedroom to store his stuff. He had over twenty guns, and there were shoes everywhere. It got late fast, and Brandy knew she had homework to do. Being that Clappa moved in, she might start doing his homework also. Brandy started getting her clothes ready to jump in the shower.

"Don't lock that door, baby. I'm jumping in the shower with you, and we have to save water, especially since we have to pay the bill!" Clappa said.

Brandy's heart started pounding as fear and nervousness took over her body. She never saw another man naked or went fully nude in front of a man, let alone take a shower with one. She wasn't sure if she should reject him or go with the flow. Even though she was a virgin, she often fantasized about having sex, but she wasn't ready to lose her virginity just yet.

Clappa pulled back the shower curtain and entered the shower. He could see Brandy was nervous, so he tried to calm her down. He reached over and grabbed her washcloth and drowned it in her favorite Dove body wash. He began to scrub her back, ass and thighs while planting kisses on her neck. Brandy's whole body started to tingle, and her pussy began to get wet. A man had never touched her in such a way, and she loved it.

Brandy didn't know if she wanted him to keep going or to stop. Clappa turned her around to face him, but she was so shy that she kept her head down the whole time. Her eyes grew wide once she saw Clappa's hard dick.

"I'm not ready for that," she said.

Clappa paid Brandy no mind and kept kissing her all over her body. When he reached her nipples, her knees got weak, her clit throbbed, and cream was coming down her legs. The feeling in her body felt so great, she never wanted it to end. Clappa got on his knees and put one of her legs over his shoulder. Her orgasm started to build up, sending waves of ecstasy through her body. She gripped the shower rod as tight as she could and released her juices in his mouth. She wanted to scream out in pure pleasure but was afraid her mother would hear.

After the shower, they headed to the bedroom. Clappa was turned on by Brandy. He wanted to taste more of her. He didn't care if he couldn't have sex with her; pleasing Brandy was his mission. He threw her down on the bed and went to work. He slowly kissed her down on the bed and went to work. He slowly kissed her, making a trail down her clit, trembling as she reached her climax. She put the pillow over her face to let out moans and screams she's been holding back. After squirting in Clappa's face, her body went limp. Clappa removed the pillow from her face to see her, and she was sound asleep. Clappa laughed, kissed her forehead, and laid next to her.

CHAPTER THREE

Graduation came around fast, and Clappa and Black did it big. Clappa rented an all-black Bentley truck. Black settled for the all-white one, and everybody was Guccied down from head to toe. Despite what happened in the past, China and Chiquita partied with Brandy and the rest of the crew. Black pulled some strings and rented out the whole Staples Center. They had the entire school there. Everybody partied and enjoyed themselves until the sun came up.

"Damn baby, I can't believe the sun is out," Brandy said.

"Yea, I'm tired as hell right now. My feet are killing me in these Gucci loafers," Clappa replied.

"Well, you can't go to sleep. I have one more surprise for you."

"This shit better be good because a nigga is tired, baby."

When Clappa pulled in the driveway, Brandy jumped out the truck and ran in the house, leaving the door open behind her.

"What the hell does this girl got up her sleeve?" Black asked as he entered the house. "Brandy? Brandy, where you at? I don't like this game."

Brandy came from the bathroom wearing nothing but fishnet stockings and pasties covering her nipples. Clappa's mouth dropped when he saw her curvy body. He dropped his bags and rushed over to her, and began kissing her. Clappa's excitement made his dick instantly hard, and he wanted Brandy bad. He was like a dog in heat, and he couldn't control himself. While kissing her, he tried to take off his clothes, but his eagerness wouldn't allow him.

"Relax, Baby, let me take care of you," she said, then pushed him down on the bed.

She grabbed and pressed play. The sound of R. Kelly began softly playing through the speakers. She began to dance with Clappa, making her butt cheeks bounce one cheek at a time. Clappa's dick felt like it was about to explode as Brandy continued to tease him.

"Damn baby, why you teasing me like this?"

Brandy giggled and kept on performing. The way she moved her body had Clappa stuck in a trance. She climbed on top of him and began to kiss him, staring at his lips and slowly working her way down. She licked his chest while slowly stroking his dick, making sure it was at full attention before she went to work. Clappa was so aroused he had to keep himself from busting a nut on himself. Brandy pulled out his rock-hard manhood and wrapped her perfect lips around the head of his dick. Brandy has seen porn before, so she knew to keep it wet and watch her teeth.

Clappa let Brandy get a few more strokes in and then took control, because she didn't have any skills in the dick sucking department. He laid her on her back and dove head first into her pussy, eating away and sending Brandy into another world. Her body shook uncontrollably as she reached her climax. Clappa licked her juices from his face then climbed on top of her, slowly entering her tight virgin pussy. Brandy couldn't hold back her screams. She didn't care if her mom was in the house or not. The mixture of pleasure and pain had her feeling like she was floating on a cloud. Clappa kept a good pace making sure to not overdo it and hurting her.

"I love you, baby," Brandy called out as her eyes rolled in the back of her head.

After Clappa came, they cleaned up the blood and went for round two.

It had been two weeks since Clappa took Brandy's virginity, and all the couple wanted to do was stay in the room and have sex. Brandy agreed to let Clappa buy some porn so they could watch together and learn new moves. Brandy still hadn't found a job, and Clappa's robbery money was running extremely low. The couple owed Brandy's mother over a thousand dollars and had no clue where they would get the money. Things went from sugar to shit really fast.

"How was the Job interview, baby?" Brandy asked as she closed her laptop when Clappa walked in.

"They told me the same thing they told you. Not a fucking thing. What did you do all day?"

"I was on the internet filling out job apps all day. I have been trying, baby. Oh yeah, Black called and said if you need anything to give him a call. He's down in Miami."

"What the hell he doing in Miami? And why the fuck is he telling you to tell me if I need anything to call him? You better not be telling that nigga my business!"

"I swear I haven't baby!"

"I heard he been hitting banks with a few niggas and them niggas been eating. I might give that nigga a call, but where were you at last night?"

"I was with China and Chiquita. We got drunk and I

lost track of time!"

"Since when you start chilling with them hoes?"

"Graduation."

"Yeah, let me find out," Clappa said suspiciously. "You shouldn't trust them."

"Why, because you use to fuck em?"

"We not gonna take it there, Brandy. That was before we got together, so let's drop that. I had a long day, and I need some of your famous services."

"That's not a problem baby, I got you as soon as I come back," Brandy said as she headed for the front door.

She left Clappa sitting there with his dick in his hand.

"If you want all that to happen, I'm going to need an extra five-hunnit," China said as she stood next to Chiquita and Brandy holding a bottle of Rose.

"If I'm going to pay you bitches twenty-five-hunnit, ya better put on a show!" the trick said as he counted out the money.

Brandy snatched the money out of his hands and began to count it while China poured Champagne in Chiquita's ass and socked it out. China pulled out a twelve-inch strap on and fucked Chiquita until her pussy and asshole were gape. That freaky shit had the trick acing crazy. He pulled out more money and threw it like he was at a strip club while China and Chiquita put on a show. Brandy sat in the back, feeling guilty that she'd been keeping secrets from Clappa.

"You want this sweet pussy?" Chiquita whispered as she cat-walked her way over to the trick.

"Yes, please give it to me," he said as he pulled out his dick.

Chiquita placed his hard rock shaft in her mouth, and slurping sounds filled the air as she deep throated his dick. China climbed on top of him and began to ride his face.

"Eat this pussy, you dirty little nigga!" she yelled while grinding on his face.

The shit talking that China was doing turned the trick all the way on, and he exploded inside the condom. Chiquita pulled the dick out of her mouth, stared at it for a second, and kissed it before she stood to her feet. China continued to grind his face until she made his beard look like a glazed doughnut. The trick sat there with a massive smile across his face and sweat beads sitting by his hairline. Brandy looked in disgust as everybody cleaned themselves and got dressed. She couldn't believe what she just witnessed.

"Ya bitches hurry the hell up! I don't have all day," Brandy said as she waited by the front door.

"Damn, Brandy, why you trippin? You know we gotta get our shit together before we leave," China said as she rushed out of the hotel room.

"And you know we gotta make sure the customer

is satisfied. We don't need these crybaby ass niggas reporting back to Black saying they didn't have a good time," Chiquita added.

When the three reached Brandy's car, Brandy gave them the two thousand and kept the five hundred for herself. It was hard hiding money from Clappa, but Brandy had plans to move the two out of South Central, and if she had to bend some corners to do it, then it was getting done. Nothing was going to stand in the way of her future.

Brandy dropped China and Chiquita off at the Harlem Western Inn. As she's pulling out of the parking lot, her guilty conscious was getting the best of her, and she wasn't sure how she would tell Clappa about the double life she's been living.

"I don't care if that nigga gets mad, shit he doesn't even have any money, so somebody has to take care of us"

She was trying to make herself feel better about the situation. Nothing could make her feel better because guilt was eating at her, so she turned on the music to avoid the voices in her head.

When she arrived home, she found Clappa sound asleep in their bed. Tears started to pour from her eyes as she watched her man sleep.

He looks so innocent, she thought. Brandy dropped her bags and got ready to take a nice hot shower. After her shower, she bumped into her mother and spilled her glass of vodka all over the floor. Her motherly instincts kicked in, and she knew something was wrong with her daughter.

"What's wrong baby, why are you crying? Is that lil nigga putting his hands on you?"

"No, it's ok Mom."

"So, what's wrong? Strong women like us don't cry very often."

"I... I... it's nothing, momma. I Swear!"

"Hold up now. I know I haven't been much a parent, but I'm your mother, and I deserve to know what's wrong with my daughter."

"Can we talk in your room?" Brandy asked.

"Yea, baby, that's not a problem. Let's go."

When they stepped inside her mother's room, Brandy was shocked by all the animal print carpet and bedspreads. There were video cameras and dildos everywhere. When Brandy sat on her bed, she tried to balance on the waterbed.

"Wow, mom, this is crazy! I never knew your room was like this."

"That's because I never let you in here. Now, what's with you?"

"Well, you know I love Clappa, right?"

"I hope you love him; you got his lil funky ass in my house eating up the food. You better love him."

"Well, I've been keeping secrets from him."

"Ah hell no, Brandy! We taking ya ass to the clinic right now. You're too young for a baby."

"No, ma, I'm not pregnant."

"Oh god, child, you scared me. So, what's going on? Are you seeing another man? Let me tell you when I was with ya father, I would bounce."

"Huh, no, Mom! I'm not seeing another man. I...I...I love Clappa. I would never have an affair. I've been helping a couple of friends of mine handle some business."

"Child, I know you not out there selling drugs!"

"No, mom, would you listen to me? Two girls I went to school with be turning out tricks, and they pay me to watch over them."

"Are you fucking any of the tricks?"

"Not at all!"

"So, what's the big deal?"

"I haven't told him, and he thinks I'm broke when I've been making five hundred every time I go on a trip with them. I want to tell him, but I don't want him to look at me funny."

"Child listen, if he's broke and you're taking care of everything, it's nothing his ass can say or do. I thought you had a serious problem."

"So, should I tell him?"

"That's up to you. The less he knows, the less drama,

so if you care about him, keep ya mouth shut. Now get out of my room and come back when you have some real problems."

CHAPTER FOUR

While Clappa was out filling job applications, Brandy was on the other side of town playing security for China and Chiquita. Noon started to roll around fast, so Clappa decided to call it a day and spend some time with his girl. When he pulled up to his street, he saw Brandy's mother pulling out the driveway, so he kept driving, praying she didn't spot him. When Brandy's mother reached the corner, he doubled back and headed into the house.

"China. China, what's good, baby? I'm home," he called out as he rushed to the bedroom.

To his surprise, China wasn't home.

Damn, where is she? he thought as he pulled out his phone to call her, only to receive her voicemail.

"Ring, Ring, Ring"

"Hello."

"Black, what's good, cuzz?"

"Damn, homie, I been tryna hit ya up; what's up with you cuzz?"

"I've been trying to get a job; I'm broke and disgusted."

"A job? Listen, cuzz, I need you. You're the only one I can trust".

"On crip. I'm not on it."

"Stay broke then nigga, but whenever you get tired of that, you know my number."

"I've been chilling."

"Well, chilling don't pay the bills nigga! Just come check me. I'm out here in Miami right now. I'll pay for your plane ticket in a few days. Just make sure you come."

"Aight cuzz."

"Imma call once the ticket is paid for."

"I need some money for my pockets, cuzz. Shit is on E."

"Call Chiquita and tell her to give you five. That should hold you until you need to come here."

After the call with Black, Clappa started pacing the floor, trying to figure out what he will do with the five hundred dollars. He knew that wasn't enough to pay Brandy's mom, so he had no intentions of letting her know about it. While he was trying to get his thoughts together, he stumbled across Brandy's purse. His heart was telling him to search it, but his trust for Brandy made him say fuck it. Instead, he decided to call her.

"Ring, ring, ring."

"Hey, baby, how did the job hunting go?" Brandy asked in an excited tone.

"I tried calling you earlier but you didn't pick up."

"I'm sorry, baby, I might have been out of service."

"Well, where are you?"

"China wanted me to put some weave in her hair, so I said fuck it because we need the money," she lied.

"Aight, well I have to make some moves, and I won't be home until 7:30 or 8 pm."

"Ok, baby, be safe."

When Clappa hung up the phone, his mind started racing a million miles per minute. He couldn't figure out why Brandy became so cool with China and Chiquita. It was beginning to make him think suspiciously about her. He didn't understand how she could go from being ready to kill them to be so buddy-buddy with them. Clappa sat on the bed and began to roll a blunt when he saw Brandy's purse again.

"Fuck it," he said out loud as he went to search the purse. He dumped all the contents on the bed and saw two boxes of condoms, tic-tacs, and eighteen-hundred in cash. Clappa's blood started boiling as he held on to the box of condoms.

"Why the fuck she got condoms."

He put everything back in her purse to make it seem as if he never searched her bag. He was unsure what to do, but he knew the first thing he must do was meet up with Chiquita and pick up the five hundred that Black told him to get.

"Bitch, you need to hurry the fuck up! You got me out here all day. I got shit I need to do," Brandy yelled through the door while China screams in passion over the music that was being played. Brandy began to send Clappa a text, knowing he would be pissed off if she came home late again.

"Damn girl, why you trippin like that? You know how these two fools get whenever they get a taste of this good pussy," China said while fixing her clothes.

"Listen, I'm not tryna hear all that shit. I got a man I have to tend to! I can't be running these streets with ya hoe ass!"

"Damn girl, why you coming at me like that?"

"I'm sorry, China, let's just go."

Seeing the condoms in any Brandy's bag had Clappa's blood boiling. He was speeding to Chiquita's Place. 50 Cents Many Men blared through his speakers while he smoked a blunt. His phone began to ring and Brandy's name popped up on the screen, but he sent it straight to voicemail. He wasn't in the mood for whatever she had to say. All he wanted was the five-hundred Chiquita had for him and the trip to Miami. When Clappa arrived in front of the Harlem Western Inn, he sat in the parking lot and smoked the rest of his blunt He needed time to get his thoughts together.

"Knock, Knock, Knock"

"Come In," Chiquita called from the back room.

"Where you at, girl?"

"In the tub."

Clappa entered the hotel room, looking around to make sure nobody was going to pop out on him. As Clappa looked around, all he saw were high heels and fishnet stockings all over the floor.

"Damn, how does she walk in these?" he said as he examined one of the heels.

The smell of Bed, Bath and Beyond kept up his nose. Then he noticed the bathroom door was ajar.

"Chiquita, what's up? I gotta make moves," Clappa called out.

"Come in here, I know you're not scared, ha."

When Clappa entered the bathroom, Chiquita was laid in a bubble bath, sipping on a glass of Remy. The radio played R&B slow jams, and the volume was perfect, just enough to set a relaxing mood. Chiquita grabbed a handful of bubbles and blew them at Clappa.

"The money is out there on the dresser, five-hunnit. Just like Black said."

"Bitch, don't ever talk to me like that again," Clappa said right after he backhanded her.

"I'm sorry," she said as she chased after him as he began to walk out of the bathroom. "I miss you, Clappa! You don't have to act so funny now that you're with Brandy. I know how to keep a secret."

When Clappa heard Brandy's name, it sent him into a rage. He rushed back to her, shook her back in the bathroom. He slapped blood out of her mouth. Then pushed her back into the tub. He began to hold her head under the water, attempting to drown her. Clappa let her come up for air then spit in her face. He forced her head back in the water, this time holding her there longer than the first time. He let her up for some more air and pulled her out of the tub by her hair, dragging her all the way to the living room.

"Bitch, tell me everything! I know you know something about Brandy. If you lie, I'm going to put a bullet in your fucking head."

"Is that what this is about? Brandy? That bitch ain't no better than me. She plays our security when we go on dates. She makes sure we get our money, and nobody hurts us."

"So, she pimping ya?"

"No, Black is our pimp."

"Black?" He asked with a confused look.

"Yea, Black. Ya right-hand man. He's our pimp. He

hired Brandy to keep an eye on us. I guess she was crying broke to the nigga, so he gave her a job."

"Why the fuck wouldn't Black tell me?"

Chiquita could see the pain and hurt in his eyes, but even more, she saw an opportunity, and she took it. She knew Clappa was in a vulnerable stage right now. So, she began to feed him lies.

Look, Clappa, I know you love Brandy, but she is a hoe, just like me."

She began to move close to him.

"Before she became our security, she went on a few dates with China and me. As soon as you took her virginity, she wanted to explore more dick, and being that she was crying broke to Black all the time made him put her on. Black didn't want to at first, but Brandy was so thirsty for dick she practically forced him to put her down. Out of respect for you, he stopped sending her on dates and made her security. I'm sorry, Clappa, but I see you really love that girl, and you deserve to know the truth, baby."

While Chiquita was talking, she slithered her way towards Clappa. After every few words, she would plant a kiss on his neck. She puts her hand under his shirt and begins to rub his chest. Her touch made his dick hard. When she saw a bulge in his pants grow, she knew she had him trapped in her web.

"You don't need her baby, let me take care of you,"

she said while unbuckling his belt.

She pulled his dick out then twirled her tongue around the tip before planting a few kisses on it.

"Quita stop," he said.

He wanted to stop her, but all the memories of all their old wild experiences started to play in his head. Chiquita looked up to see he was in ecstasy and began to deep throat his dick. She had no gag reflexes, so it was easy for her to make his shaft disappear and reappear in and out of her mouth. Clappa came to his climax and unloaded his seeds in her mouth, and she didn't hesitate to swallow while staring him in the eyes.

"Remember that?"

"How could I forget?" Clappa replied while pulling up his pants. "Where you said the money was at?"

"Damn, so you just gonna leave? It's on the dresser."

When Brandy arrived home, she noticed Clappa wasn't there and wanted to surprise him with a candle-lit dinner. She prepared an eight-ounce T-bone steak, macaroni and cheese, with a side of broccoli. Everything was perfect, and she couldn't wait for Clappa to return home. When Brandy changed her clothes, she noticed her Gucci bag sitting on the floor and deciding to go through it. Before she could finish, she heard Clappa enter the house and tried to rush downstairs to meet him.

"Hey, baby," she said, trying to catch her breath. "I cooked us some food. It's cold now because I thought you would have been home earlier. Sit down while I warm up the food."

While Brandy warmed up the food, Clappa assumed she was up to something, so he watched her with a suspicious look in his eyes. When she returned to the table with plates, Clappa ate in silence. She had no clue why he was acting this way, so she decided to break the silence.

"I paid my mom."

Clappa gives her a fake grin, finished his food, put his plate in the sink, and went upstairs to the shower. Brandy sat at the table confused and didn't know what to do, so she washed the dishes, went upstairs, and jumped in the shower with Clappa.

"Can I join?" she asked while she stood there naked.

Clappa ignored her question and continued to wash up. Brandy couldn't figure out why he was acting this way, but she entered the shower without his permission and began to wash his back. Clappa turned around to face Brandy, and the look of evil was in his eyes. He pushed her head down to his dick. She didn't think twice and began to suck his dick quickly, bringing him to climax. Clappa pulled out and busts on her face.

Damn, he never did any disrespectful shit like this before! she thought as she wiped the cum from her face.

"Bend over," Clappa demanded.

Brandy stood up and bent over, making sure to grab her ankles just like he taught her. Clappa took his dick and rammed it in her asshole, causing excruciating pain to the point where she felt like she wanted to pass out. When Clappa reached his climax, he left her in the shower.

"I'm going to Miami," he said as he exits the bathroom.

CHAPTER FIVE

As Clappa stepped off the plane, the bright Miami sun caused him to put his hand over his eyebrows. He was happy to be away from L.A and away from Brandy. All the thinking he was doing made him feel as if he was about to lose his mind. A trip to Miami was precisely what he needed. Clappa started looking around for Black when he spotted him hopping out of an all-white Bentley GT. His mind was blown when he saw all the iced-out jewelry he had on.

"What's good, cuzz?" Black said as he hugged Clappa.

The hug felt fake, and it's because Clappa had a few things he needed to get off his chest, but now wasn't the time.

"Damn, Cuzz, this ya ride?" Clappa asked as he entered the Bentley.

"It's about to be yours soon," Black replied.

The two drove with the windows rolled down, enjoying the Miami weather, smoking. The gated mansion with a six-car garage full of exotic cars, grass that was greener than a football field, and a water fountain in the front yard.

"I know this ain't ya crib," Clappa said in an excited tone."

"I wish. It's this lil bitch's crib I fuck with. Her dad is in the oil business, so he spoils the lil freak bitch."

"So, this where are we staying?"

"Yea cuzz, Imma show you ya room. You need to get some sleep. I want you well rested when we go make this move."

"What about the girl, she not goin to be on no bullshit?"

"She took a plane to Japan, so the house and cars are ours until we decide to leave."

When Clappa entered the house, he ran around like a kid at a candy store. He was so happy to be in such luxury, he didn't know how to act. He ran to the bar and poured himself a drink. His excitement took over, and he forgot all about getting rest.

"You a lucky nigga," Clappa said as he poured a shot."

"Nah, cuzz, I wouldn't call it luck. I just put myself in the right position, that's all."

"If that's what you call it."

"Get some rest. Imma makes a few moves. I'll be back later. Don't break anything."

The liquor began to kick in, and Clappa felt that it was starting to kick in and get the best of him. His heart wanted him to call Brandy, but his pride and ego wouldn't let him. Between the plane ride and the mixture of weed and liquor, made Clappa pass out. He tried to make it to the guest room, but his wobbly legs caused him to do otherwise, and he fell asleep on the couch.

"Oh, yes, fuck me, daddy!"

"Whose pussy is this?" Black said.

"It's all yours, baby. All yours, ohhh."

The sound of screams and moans filled the air and woke Clappa from his sleep with a rock hard dick.

"Damn, he knocking that pussy out the frame" he thought as he grabbed his dick and headed to the bathroom.

Clappa put his hand on the wall to help him keep his balance as he took a piss. He had a crazy hangover, and the only thing to cure was to take another shot or smoke a blunt.

The sound of a knock at the door startled Clappa as he washed his hands.

"Hold on a minute," he yelled out.

He threw some water on his face and exited the

bathroom. When he opened the door, to his surprise, he saw Brandy, China, and Chiquita all standing there half-naked. His heart dropped when he noticed Brandy standing there, and she dyed her hair blonde.

"What the fuck is going on?"

"Move nigga! After all that good dick, I have to pee," China said as she pushed Clappa to the side and rushed to the toilet.

"Brandy, what the fuck you doing here?" Clappa asked.

"The same thing you doing here. I'm getting paid."

"We all tryna get paid," added Chiquita.

Clappa's head began to pound as he soaked up what was goin on. He couldn't believe his girl was in Miami with the same two hoes which had her running the streets late at night. He gave her the benefit of the doubt when he saw the condoms and tic-tac's in her purse, but seeing her in Miami with China and Chiquita made things clear.

"Where the fuck is Black?" he asked as he dragged Brandy to the master bedroom. Clappa saw red and wanted some answers on why his girl was half-naked in Miami with two hoes. He was ready to kill everybody in the house. He felt betrayed, and Clappa was big on loyalty. He continued to drag Brandy by her hair pushing every few feet to kick her in the ribs and call her a hoe.

"Stop hitting like that!" China and Chiquita yelled

out.

"Fuck you bitches! It's ya fault she out here hoeing."

Clappa left Brandy on the floor, holding her side and gasping for air while he took off and rushed to his luggage to retrieve his famous 9mm. He ran back to Brandy and saw China and Chiquita on their knees trying to cater to her. He put a bullet in the back of China's head and ended her life immediately.

"Please, Clappa, don't do this," Chiquita tried to plead with him. "It's not our fault Black..."

Before she could finish her sentence, a bullet entered her eye and exited the back of her head, quickly ending her life. Clappa wiped the blood from his face and gave Brandy the devil look. Fear took over her body, and words couldn't come out of her mouth. All she could do was cry and gasp for air.

"Bitch, stand the fuck up!" he said as he pulled her to her feet by her hair.

Clappa was on a rampage and wasn't leaving Miami until he got answers, and everybody in the house was dead.

He kicked in Black's door and saw him staring out the window with a blunt in his hand. Clappa stood there holding Brandy by the hair with his gun pointed at Black. He wanted to shoot Black in the back of the head, but he wanted answers first.

"So, this how are we doing shit, huh cuzz?"

"It's all business, cuzz. I wanted to tell you in L.A, but you was so stuck up under Brandy's ass, you couldn't see what was going on right under your nose," replied Black.

"I knew you since kindergarten, homie! You were was supposed to tell me my girl was out here hoeing."

"I told that bitch to tell you! She cried broke, so I put the hoe on and gave her a job. Nothing more, nothing less."

"But you was just in here fucking her!" Clappa said, gripped his gun even tighter.

"Well, what pimp don't fuck their hoes? I have to make sure that pussy still works. I flew you out here to let you know what ya bitch been doing, and now that the cat is out the bag, we can get to this money and not have to hide anything from each other."

Clappa couldn't believe that he's been in a circle of lies between his best friend and his girl. What hurt the most is that he had planned on making Brandy his wife. The betrayal and pain that he felt was unbearable. He stared at Brandy while she was knelt down at his right side. He slowly raised his gun and put a bullet in the top of Brandy's head. Her body instantly went limp, and a tear dropped from Clappa's eyes as he watched blood pour out of her head. He switched his attention to Black and raised his gun at Black. He got on his knees and begged for his life.

"Come on, cuzz, we brothers, you don't have to do this."

"We were brothers until you betrayed me," replied Clappa as his grip on the gun got tighter.

"Clappa! Clappa! Clappa!" Black cried out. "Clappa! Clappa!"

Clappa opened his eyes and saw Black shaking his leg calling his name. He looked around as if he was lost. That's when he let out a deep sigh and realized he was dreaming.

"Damn cuzz, you goin sleep all day? I went shopping for you and put ya clothes in the closet. Go get dressed we, going clubbing."

Clappa staggered to the shower. He had to wash off all the alcohol he sweated out from the nap he took. Scenes of his dream kept playing back in his head. He ignored his thoughts and finished showering. When he stepped into the guest room, he couldn't believe how big it was. He opened the closet and saw all the latest designer clothes. Clappa opted for a pair of Gucci jeans with a matching jacket and a pair of Gucci sneakers to put the outfit together.

He headed downstairs to meet Black on the phone. He tried to eavesdrop on his conversation to make sure he wasn't talking to Brandy, but he turned around before he got another word out. He looked Clappa up and down, and gave him a thumbs up.

Back in LA, Brandy was lost without her man. He hadn't called since he left for Miami. She had no money after paying her mother, and Clappa took all the money in her purse. Brandy decided to call Chiquita, but got the voice mail. So, she tried China, and she picked up on the first ring.

"Hey, what's up, girl? How ya doing?" China said

"What's up girl? How ya doing??

"We on a date right now."

"Is that right? I tried calling Quita, but she ain't pick up."

"Yea, she on some other shit."

"Ya didn't need my services today?"

"Quita said we could do it on our own."

"Put that bitch on the phone!"

"What?" Chiquita snapped.

"So, that's how we doing business now?"

"Listen, Brandy, it is what it is. We don't need to pay you to stand around and look like a statue. You better get with the program and use what you got to get this money."

"Bitch fuck you! I'm goin see ya stank ass around, don't worry."

"Click."

"This spot is jumping," Clappa said as he yelled over

the music.

"This is how they play out here. You see how all these hoes are half-naked?"

"What's up cuzz, I know you didn't bring me out here to party the whole time, so what's good?" Clappa asked, getting straight to the point.

"I got a lick that could set us up for life. These niggas out here slow as hell."

"So, break it down to me."

"Check it, you know China and Chiquita well. I got them fucking these two tricks. One is a jeweler, and the other is a manager at Bank of America. We will literally catch these niggas with their pants down, take their ass to their establishment, and get the money. It's easy as one, two, and three."

Clappa sat there and let Black's words sink in as he thought about the life-changing money they could possibly make. Clappa was used to robbing the local drug dealers and the gamblers' shock around the way. He never attempted to pull off a job like this. He couldn't believe China and Chiquita were going to have parts of the robberies. Hearing their names made his blood boil, and he felt like now was the perfect time to ask Black about brandy.

"Aight Cuzz, I'm in." He said as he dapped Black up. "I gotta ask you something."

"Shoot," Black replied.

"What's up with you and Brandy?"

"What you mean Cuzz?'

"Don't play stupid."

"I see she still hasn't told you. Well, one day I was calling your phone, and you weren't picking up, so I tried her phone, and when she answered, she said you were out there job hunting. Then she started crying about how ya was broke and, blah, blah, blah, so I put her down, but she was supposed to tell you."

"Well, how you expect a woman to tell her man that she's selling pussy."

"Selling pussy?" Black began to laugh. "Brandy aint selling pussy. I would never do that to you. I know how you love that girl. She's security for China and Chiquita, that's all. What made you think she was selling pussy?"

"Chiquita told me."

"Nigga you can't believe that hoe."

CHAPTER SIX

China and Chiquita's scream powered the music that was playing. The performance they were putting on was excellent. China let the jeweler hit her from the back while she had a vibrator in her ass. At the same time, Chiquita was riding the banker like a cowgirl. Clappa and Black sat in the hotel's parking lot, waiting for the signal to make their move. Clappa tried to calm his nerves with a blunt, but he couldn't hide the sweat dripping from his head.

"Nobody gonna get hurt, right?" asked Clappa.

"As long as these niggas cooperate, everything should be good."

Twenty minutes later, the music stopped, and the lights went off and then back on again. Black pulled the ski mask over his face then cocked his gun. He looked over at Clappa to see he was stuck in the same position.

"Come on, cuzz, it's time to move," Black said.

Clappa put his fear aside and thought about his future with Brandy. He pulled his ski mask down and pulled out his 9mm. Black kicked the door in and made everybody get on the ground. They roughed up China and Chiquita to make it look real. Clappa slapped Chiquita with all his might for all the lies she told him. They gagged and blindfolded them so they couldn't see what was going on. China and Chiquita stayed in the hotel room and cleaned everything up to make it look like nothing ever happened.

"Shut the fuck up before I kill you!" Clappa yelled at one of the crying tricks.

They figured they would hit the bank first because it was closer to the hotel. While driving to the bank, they saw flashing lights, and Clappa began to panic.

"Ok, listen to me, Motha fucka! If you want to live, you will do exactly as I say. We going go in this bank and you goin to put in the alarm code, then ya punk ass is gonna take me to the vault and we are going to fill up these duffle bags, then you goin help me carry them back to the car. Are we clear?" Black asked.

"Mmmmm," the banker muttered.

"Stay in the car with him. If he moves, shoot em. This should be quick. I'll be in and out." Black said to Clappa.

When Black exited the car, Clappa really started to panic. Here he was in Miami with some Jewish jeweler tied and gagged in the back seat. They were the only car in the bank's parking lot, and it was three in the morning. If a cop drove by, they would for sure pull up to the car to see what was going on. The jeweler was trying to say something, but Clappa ignored him.

"Mmmmm"

"Nigga, shut the fuck up!"

"Mmmm."

Clappa grew frustrated and pistol-whipped the jeweler, causing blood to leak from his head.

"Now shut the fuck up, because the next time I'mma put a bullet in ya head."

He turned back to the car, holding two duffle bags apiece.

Damn, he really pulled it off, he thought as Black loaded the trunk with the duffle bags.

"Why he bleeding cuzz?"

"He kept trying to talk, but I think he got the message now."

"Listen cuzz, get in and out, and take the jewelry if this nigga plays any games. If he starts acting too crazy, pop his stupid ass," Black said as they sat outside the jewelry store.

"I got this."

Clappa's heart was pounding as he began to think

about all the possible things that could go wrong. His palms began to sweat, and sweat beads formed on his forehead once again. He wanted to back out, but he came too far to turn back now, and he desperately needed money. The jeweler tried to speak again. Black looked back at him then over to Clappa and gave him a look as to say, "Make sure you handle this." Clappa and Black both got out of the car. Black got in the driver's seat while Clappa dragged the jeweler out of the back seat.

"Do as I say, and I won't hurt you; it's that simple. Now push in the security code."

The jeweler complied with Clappa's commands and put in the security code. Clappa rushed into the store dragging the jeweler along with him. He started grabbing jewelry from the showcase, filling his duffle bag with all kinds of jewelry. Clappa headed towards the back of the store to go for big money, but when he turned around, he saw the jeweler trying to make a run for it, so he shot him in the back.

"Nigga, I told ya stupid ass to stay cool, now look what you made me do!"

Clappa dragged him to the back where the safe was and made him put in the combination. When the safe was open, Clappa's face lit up at the sight of all the shiny diamonds and neatly stacked money. In three swipes, he emptied the safe leaving nothing behind. Black saw

Clappa exit out the store with a duffle bag and dragging the jeweler at the same time. He rushed out of the car to help Clappa.

"I heard a shot go off; what happened?" he asked as he loaded the jeweler in the backseat.

"He tried to make a run for it, so I popped him."

Clappa and Black drove all the way to Tampa to dump the car and two the tricks on a back road. They were pretty sure the jeweler would bleed out and die, so Black had intentions of killing them both, but Clappa stopped him. Five minutes after they dumped the car, China and Chiquita were up in all Black Chevy Tahoe. China started rolling blunts, while Black and Clappa loaded the trunk with duffle bags. They smoked and cruised all the way to Jacksonville so they could stop at a cheap motel to count up all the money.

"That's a total of 3.1 million. We going to give these hoes five-hunnit-thousand to split and a Rolex and send them on their way. We are not goin to tell them about the diamonds and the rest of the jewelry; that shit is for us," Black said as he separated everything.

"Aight, cuzz, I'm with it. I still can't believe we pulled that shit off. What you goin do with ya money?"

"I'm not sure, but it's goin to be something big."

"Brandy's been talking about leaving L.A a lot, so that's the first thing I'm going to do."

"Yea, cuzz, you need to get out of there ASAP."

"Ma," Brandy called from the bathroom.

"Damn, Brandy, what the hell is it? I'm busy."

"My stomach hurts, and I've been spotting blood. I need you to take me to the doctor because something is wrong."

Brandy's mother helped Brandy to the car, and they drove to the hospital. She knew what was wrong with Brandy but didn't want to say anything. She would rather have the doctor tell her she was having a miscarriage. Brandy's mother had plenty of abortions and miscarriages to know what stomach pain and blood spots meant. Brandy was the only child but would have had way more brothers and sisters if it wasn't for her mom's reckless ways.

Sitting in the waiting room seemed like forever for Brandy. When her name was finally called, her anxiety started to kick in. After being told she had a miscarriage, she was heartbroken. All she wanted was Clappa, and he was being an asshole to her. She pulled out her cellphone and dialed his number, only to get his voicemail. She cried the whole way home while her mom tried to assure her that everything would be fine. Brandy ignored her words and continued to sob. It was more than the miscarriage that was bothering her.

"Stop crying, child, it's ok, all you have to do is try

again. That's all, it's not that big of a deal, baby."

She looked at her mother with evil eyes as she continued to speak. She wasn't the best person to take advice from. Brandy was ready to snap at the dumb things she was saying. When they arrived home, Brandy went straight to her room and tried calling Clappa, but still no answer.

"Just fly Brandy out here, cuzz. I don't know why you want to leave," Black said as he drove Clappa to the greyhound station.

"I need to surprise her. I haven't spoken to her since I left. I want to pop up and see her reaction."

"What if she has a new man or some shit?"

"Fuck it, I got money now. I can buy a new bitch if I really wanted to."

"How long you plan on being in LA?" Black asked as he parked in the parking lot of the Greyhound station."

"I got a few loose ends to tighten up, and I'm coming back down here."

Clappa and Black said their goodbyes and went their separate ways. Clappa paid for his ticket and took a seat, and began to eat lunch when he heard gunshots going off. Everybody rushed to the window to see what was going on, but Clappa stayed put because he knew it was nothing that involved him. He pulled out his phone to call Brandy, but surprising her with all the cash made him change his mind. So he put his phone back in his pocket and headed to the bathroom. There were a few arcade games by the bathroom, so he made a mental note to play the new Street Fighter on the way back to his seat. He went inside a stall instead of using the urinal. He wanted to look at the possessions that were in the duffle bag. The diamonds shine bright, and he couldn't stop smiling at his accomplishment. All the excitement was soon dampened by a knock on the bathroom stall door.

"Hold on one minute," Clappa said as he slowly zipped up his duffle bag.

"Knock, Knock, Knock."

"I said hold the fuck..."

Clappa words were cut short when he opened the door to see five men standing there with bulletproof vests that read FBI across the chest. His first thoughts were to run, but he was surrounded and had nowhere to go.

"Antwan Jackson, you're under arrest," the agent said as he hand-cuffed Clappa. His world stopped when he saw FBI on the vest. He knew it was for a serious matter whenever they came. Clappa's whole life flashed before his eyes, and the walk to the squad car seemed like forever. When he got outside, he saw Black lying on the floor with his pistol in his hand and filled with bullet holes. He couldn't believe his best friend was dead, and he let out a few tears. There were flashing lights everywhere, news reporters were trying to get the story, and other FBI agents were sitting around talking while Clappa walked with his head down to the squad car. Everything was going in slow motion at this point. The FBI agents drove him to the courthouse. They gave him nothing to eat and had him sitting in the dirty bullpen with no shoelaces or belts. He paced the floor, walking back and forth until he was called to meet his lawyer. When he entered the room, his lawyer began to read his charges.

"You're looking at a lot of time, Mr. Jackson. There are only three ways you can get this over and done with. Option one is to cop out with the first offer they come with; option two is to take them to trial, which won't be good for you; and option three is to cooperate. Now, most guys go with option three…"

"Listen, if you ever disrespect me again and talk about some cooperation bullshit, we are going to have some serious problems. We are going to trial and make sure you let that be known," Clappa said interrupting his lawyer.

The whole ride to the jailhouse was all a blur. The fact that Clappa was in federal custody still seemed unreal. Black was dead, China and Chiquita were nowhere to be found, and he wasn't sure how he would tell Brandy that he's facing the rest of his life in prison. When he arrived at the jail, he decided to call her.

"You have a call from Antwan Jackson, a federal Inmate. Press five to accept the call," the operator said.

Brandy quickly pressed five, and Clappa was happy to hear her voice.

"Clappa, what the hell is going on? Baby, where are you? I'm on my way!"

"I'm in Florida. Everything went bad. I wanted everything to be perfect for you, but I fucked up. I'm sorry, baby."

"Baby, what happened?"

"Black is dead, and I'm facing the rest of my life in prison."

"Oh my God, what happened to Black?"

"It's a long story," he said, and tears started to flow. "Just make me one promise."

"Anything, baby, what is it?"

"Promise me, no matter what happens, you will always love me."

"I will always love you Clappa, nothing can change that," Brandy replied before the phone hung up.

CHAPTER SEVEN

It had been three years since Clappa got arrested, and it has been a bumpy road for him and Brandy. She had been having a hard time facing the fact that she may never get to be with Clappa again physically. She wished this was all a dream, and Clappa wished he could go back to job hunting. It's how one minute you can be on top of the world and then the next minute you're beneath it. Today was sentencing day, and Clappa was feeling confident about the verdicts. Butterflies danced around in his stomach when they called his name to see the judge.

Clappa looked around the courtroom to see who was present, and the only person there to support him was Brandy. She found a job in Florida at a nursing home, so she moved down there to be close to him. She smiled and waved at him with tears in her eyes. He smiled back and blew a kiss at her. The court was now in session and the verdict was in. Clappa looked back at Brandy one last time and mouthed the words, "I got this."

"Before I go with sentencing, do you have anything you would like to say, Mr. Jackson?"

"No man"

"Ok, so let's proceed with sentencing. Mr. Jackson, I hereby sentence you to 339 months for two counts of the Hobbs Act and one count of 924(c). Does anybody have any objections?"

"No, your honor," The lawyer and DA said at the same time.

"So, 339 months is the sentence I oppose. It's the sentence I find sufficient, but not greater than necessary, to serve the purpose of sentencing."

Brandy almost fainted when she heard what Clappa was sentenced to. Clappa tried to stay strong for Brandy, but he couldn't believe his young life was being taken away from him so fast. He didn't even know how many years 339 months were.

On the way back to jail, Clappa sat in the back of the van, quiet while all the other inmates talked about who was hot and who wasn't. His mind was blank, and all he wanted to do was to go to sleep so he could hopefully wake up from his nightmare. An image of Brandy's crying face popped in his head. He wanted to drop a tear but didn't because he had to keep his image on for the other inmates. He didn't want them thinking he was soft or something. Clappa let out a light chuckle when he thought about all the good times he and Black had.

"How much time they give you?" an inmate asked.

"Too much," Clappa replied.

When Clappa got to the jail, he went to shower. After the shower, he went straight to his cell and laid on his back, letting reality kick in. He never got to enjoy the money, so he began asking himself questions like, "Was it all worth it? Will I make it out alive?" And every question a man asks when he gets locked up. "Will my girl stay by my side?" He pulled out a pen and paper and started writing Brandy a letter. By the time he was finished, he had realized he had written her a ten-page letter.

"You good homie?" his cellie asked.

"I don't have a choice."

"I'm just checking. I've seen dudes get sentenced and start tripping when they come back to the unit."

"I'm stronger than that cuzz; I'm not going to flip out, trust me."

"Aight, homie, if you want to talk, just let me know. I'm here for you."

Three months later, he was on a plane to U.S.P Atwater.

They sent him back to his home state California. All he could think about was how in the hell Brandy was going to come to visit him. They had minor issues with his insecurities. Whenever she didn't pick up the phone, he would think she was with another man. If she missed a visit, he would write her a letter telling her to move on with her life. If she couldn't send her money and he had to miss commissary, he would call and curse her out. When Clappa arrived at Atwater, the tension was in the air. So, the first thing he did was make a shank. Everything was segregated. If you were in a gang, you stuck with your gang, and if you were neutral, you stuck with whatever state you're were from. Lockdown time came around, and Clappa wrote Brandy a letter:

Dear Brandy, 7-1-2007

Hey, my love, how is everything? I hope all is well. I decided to write you a letter before I called because I knew you would be pissed off. They sent my black ass back to California. I'm not sure why, but any shots for 16 months I can out in a transfer and move to U.S.P Coleman, or you can move back to California. Either way, I want you closer. Brandy, I want to thank you for being my rock. Without you, I'm not sure if I would be able to do this. I appreciate everything baby, I truly do. I know sometimes I can be hard to deal with, and it takes a strong woman to put up with the things I put you through. I love you more than words can explain, and I hope you know that. Love always, your everything.

Brandy was stuck between a rock and a hard place.

She loved her man, but life in Florida was going well for her. After reading Clappa's letter, she laid on her bed and cried her eyes out. She couldn't believe the love of her life was doing so much time. Flashbacks of old memories begin to play in her head, and a smile came across her face. Clappa and Brandy made some good memories, but also made a lot of bad ones. While Clappa was fighting his case for the past three years, he and Brandy had many arguments, and it drove her into the arms of another man. The love she had for him was too strong for her to leave him, so she stuck around. She could never leave Clappa, and that's why her boyfriend left her, but she wasn't mad because she could never do him dirty. While Brandy lay on her bed, she picked up a pen and paper and began to reply to his letter.

Dear Clappa, 7-8-2007

Clappa, I want you to know that no matter what happens, I will always love you. I hate that we are in a situation, but we have to make the best of it. I hope you do stay out of trouble so you can get back closer to me. I love my life out here, and I don't plan on leaving it anytime soon. You know my dream was to leave Cali, and I've finally made it. So, to answer your question, no, I'm not moving back out there; I will come to visit as much as I can. Baby, I want you to focus on us and don't get caught up in that jail nonsense. Make a plan and stick to it, because I don't have time to be moving around the whole world to visit you.

p.s. I'm coming to visit in September. Love always, your rock.

It was time to visit Clappa and Brandy was nervous; she wanted everything to be perfect. She spent well over five-hundred making sure her nails and make were on point. She hadn't been to California since she left. When she stepped off the plane, her heartbeat increased as her anxiety started to kick in. All her memories started flashing in her head, good and bad. Brandy never wanted to return back to Cali, but her man needed her and was ready to go the extra mile for the love of her life.

"Brandy Smith." Brandy's name was being called for her to enter the visiting room. She double-checked her appearance to make sure everything was on point. When she entered the visiting room, they locked eyes. She ran over to him and jumped in his arms. His grip was strong, and she could tell he had been working out. His body was tight, and his arms were busting out the sleeves of his jumper. They hugged and kissed until the guard told them to stop.

"You look so good, baby," Brandy said as she wiped her tears from her eyes.

"Yeah, baby," I'm trying to stay fit. I wanna look good for you when I come home."

"So, did you file for an appeal?" asked Brandy.

"Not yet baby, that's a process."

"Ok."

"Did you figure out if you was going to move back out here to be closer to me?"

Brandy took a deep breath and dropped her head. She knew this conversation was bound to happen. She hoped it wasn't this fast into the visit.

"You got my letter, right?"

"Yeah, but I was praying you would have changed ya mind."

"Well baby, I just got a promotion at my job, and to be honest, I didn't want to leave. The cost of living is cheap. I have a good job, and it's nice and peaceful out there. I don't hear gunshots and helicopters all day. What about the transfer you were talking about?"

"Baby, this place is a zoo; I doubt I will be able to stay out of trouble for that long."

"Well, if I mean anything to you, you will stay out of trouble," Brandy said in a snappy tone.

Brandy could feel the tension building up and wanted to change the subject. She didn't want to waste a trip all the way to California just to argue. She felt Clappa was picking at everything she did or didn't do. She wanted to walk out and leave, but instead she walked to the vending machine hoping that he would be in a better mood by the time she came back. Clappa's insecurities were getting the best of him, and he couldn't control it.

As Brandy began to walk back to the table with the food and drinks that she purchased from the vending machine, Clappa sat there with his arms crossed, and she could tell he had a lot of fight left left in him. Clappa eyed her from head to toe and could see she was getting thicker, and his mind began to play tricks on him. Everything about her was different. She even walked differently, and it made Clappa's mind wonder. What he failed to realize is that Brandy was not the same little virgin that he first met. She was a grown woman now, and all the trials and tribulations she's been through have shaped her into the woman that stood before him today.

"I got you hot wings and a sprite. They had turkey sandwiches, but they looked old and cheap."

Brandy was trying to lighten up the mood and kill the tension that was in the air. Being locked up for the past three years had turned Clappa into a heartless goon. He was so busy trying to play hard that he forgot to tell Brandy how good she looked. Clappa eyed Brandy, and the more he stared at her, the madder he got. The thought of being locked up for 339 months and not keeping track of Brandy's every move was eating him alive.

"Are you going to visit ya mom?" Clappa asked as he began to eat the food.

"Yeah, I have to see how she's doing. You know she's getting old."

"I have a question for you, and I want you to be completely honest with me," Clappa said, quickly changing the subject.

"Anything baby."

"Have you been with anybody since I been gone?"

Brandy's heart skipped two beats. She wanted to tell him the truth, but her heart wouldn't let her. She looked dead into his eyes to say to him yes, but her mouth fixed the word "no." She hated the fact that she just lied to him, but she didn't want to put him through any more stress than he already had to go through.

"So, you mean to tell me the whole time I been gone you haven't been with anybody?"

"That's exactly what I said, right?" she replied, catching an attitude. "Look, Clappa, I didn't fly out here to argue. I haven't been with anybody, and that's my word."

"I'm sorry, baby, this place is really starting to get to me. I have too much time to think, and sometimes it just gets to me. I'm sorry, baby."

Brandy felt the weight fall off her shoulders since he apologized. She would eventually tell him that there was somebody else in the picture at one point in time. The rest of the visit went well. They laughed, joked, hugged, and kissed. The clock was ticking, and the visit would soon end, and Clappa had something he wanted to get off his chest and felt like now was a perfect time.

"Baby, we been through a lot," Clappa said while he held her hands."

"Tell me about it," replied Brandy.

"And you been putting up with me since day one. Remember when I handed you my bookbag that one day?"

"Yeah, how can I forget?"

"That's where our history started. I know I have a lot of time, and it's a possibility that may never come home."

"Don't talk like that," Brandy interrupted as tears begin to well up in her eyes.

"It's true, baby, and I want to know will you marry me?"

"Yes, baby! Yes, yes, yes, I will marry you." She said in an excited tone.

CHAPTER EIGHT

Hey Brandy, a few of us co-workers are going out for drinks tonight. Why don't you join us?" the co-worker said.

"I don't know about all that, Jessica, I'm tired, and I have to be right back here at eight in the morning."

"Come on, girl, you need to get out. All you do is work and go home. You need a man."

"I have a man!" Brandy replied defensively.

"Girl, that man is in prison forever and never coming home. I salute you for trying to be faithful, but shit, you have needs. You don't miss lying in bed next to a strong man or bouncing on a nice hard dick? I can't go longer than a week without it. I'm like a cat in heat."

"Hahaha, you are so nasty, Jessica, but for your info, I've had a man since he's been gone, but it doesn't feel right. Clappa is my first love, and I never been with another man until last year, and that didn't last long because I always put Clappa first."

"Listen, girl, I hear you and everything, but come out tonight and have a drink. Derrick is going to be there, and you know he has a crush on you. I see how he acts whatever you come around."

"Huh? I ain't worried about no Derrick, and besides, he's not even my type," Brandy said while blushing.

"Just come, please?"

"I will think about it."

The days in prison were going by fast. It had been two-and-a-half months since Clappa last saw Brandy, and she made a promise that she would come to see him every three months. Ever since they got engaged, Clappa's jealousy slowly faded away, and his trust for Brandy began to grow. She never missed a phone call, and the arguing stopped. Brandy was happy to be engaged to Clappa. The thought of being loved had her excited. She was down for her man, and she wanted everybody to know, but the temptation is a bitch.

"Damn, homie, you always getting a pile of mail. Half of the mailbag is for you."

"I already to you, Clappa, but you don't want to listen to me," Banga said she he walked back to his cell.

"I don't need to join a penpal website. I got a girl. My girl is loyal, and she's been writing since day one."

"All that's cool, but she's a woman with needs, and one day she is going to weigh out her options and come to a realization that she needs her needs fulfilled."

"I hear you, but I have faith in my girl!"

"Ok, well, whenever you want me to put you on, just let me know," Banga said as he waved the stack of mail in Clappa's face.

Clappa went to his cell to ponder on what Banga was telling him. Half of him wanted to believe what he was saying, and the other half of him wanted to believe Brandy would stay. 339 months was a long time for somebody to wait for a guy that was in a maximum-security prison. He had faith in her, but he couldn't see past the time he had. He tried to block out his thoughts with music from his radio. Having a side chick wouldn't be that bad, he thought as he looked at the pen-pal brochure.

The next day, Clappa woke up feeling energized. He wanted to call Brandy as soon as he woke up, but he knew she might still be asleep in a different time zone. He rushed to Banga's cell, and as usual, he was sitting at his desk writing a letter.

"Damn homie, I see you play no games," Clappa said as he entered the cell.

"Yea, today is Thursday. I gotta get all these letters

out tonight," replied Banga.

"So, you got a little system goin on, huh?"

"Something like that."

"So, what's up? How do I get on the site?"

"Ohhh, now you want to join the game?" Banga said sarcastically.

"I slept on it, and I made up my mind."

"I see."

"You can have your family put you on this pen-pal site called I'mTrending.com, and post your ad. Just wait for some hits.

"I don't have any family and my girl won't do it."

"So fill out the brochure I gave you last week and send it off to the company with your picture and a BP-199."

Banga continued to school Clappa on how to set up winning profile on I'mTrending.com. Clappa sat there and sucked in all the information. His excitement started to grow when Banga pulled out pictures and letters from the pen-pals. He couldn't believe all the beautiful women out there who wanted to talk to incarcerated men. When Banga was done giving him the game, he rushed to his cell, made a bio, and began going through his pictures to see which ones he thought would be best for his profile.

He rushed to the mailbox and dropped the envelope.

"Now I wait," he said as he walked back to his cell.

He laid on his bed and played his music on his system that was made out of R-10 headphones. Once he started to relax and let his mind wander, Banga rushed into the cell.

"Yo, get ya knife! One of the DC niggas took off on a Mexican."

Clappa didn't have to go far to get his knife because it was in the pocket of his sweatpants. Once he jumped up, the cell door was flung open, and in came three Mexicans. Banga and Clappa rushed towards them, knives in hand, swinging for dear life, making sure they got out of the cell alive. Even though they were outnumbered, nothing was stopping them from getting out of the cell.

The scene was a bloody mess when the two made it out of the cell. The only thing that was on Clappa's mind was on was to stab anything that wasn't Africa-American. When Clappa locked in on his target, the tear gas and pepper spray slowed him down. All he heard were loud bangs, then everything went white for a minute. He was tackled to the floor and handcuffed. He held his eyes shut because the tear gas had it hard to see.

Brandy, 9-12-07

Hey baby, I hope all is well on your end because everything is all bad on my end. I'm writing because you are going to have to cancel our visit. I'm in the box right now, but it's not my fault. A riot broke out, and I had to fend for my life. It's a long story that I don't feel like giving you the details to, so please understand and don't be mad at me. Whenever they let me use the phone, I will call. I'm going to cut this letter short and wait for your reply.

Love always, your rock.

A week later, Clappa's letter arrived in Brandy's mailbox. She was more than excited to read it, so she ran into her room, jumped on her bed, and laid on her back to read the letter. She felt like a teenager in love all over again. When she saw how short the letter was, she knew something wasn't right. Her anxiety started to kick in when she read the words box and riot. Her flight was already booked to see Clappa, but now she had to cancel it. She began looking at her engagement ring and wondered how long it would last before he got killed or before she gave up.

Brandy cried herself to sleep. She wanted to reply to his letter, but was drained and tried. When she woke up, it was time to get ready for work. Clappa's letter was still on her mind while she showered, but she quickly blocked out all negative thoughts and focused on the day ahead of her. She was good at covering up her emotions, so nobody at work knew she had any real problems going on.

"Hey girl," Jessica said while she spotted Brandy.

"Hey girl, good morning." replied Brandy.

"I went and got my hair done after work. Everybody was asking last week when we went out, especially Derrick's fine ass."

"I had some family issues I had to handle. I wanted to come, but you know I put my priorities before anything."

"I respect that. Well, we are getting together again tonight and you should come. I'm not taking no for an answer."

Brandy sat and thought about it, and with everything that was going on, she needed a drink. Her mind was on Clappa, and she wondered if he was being treated right in the box. Her mind quickly shifted to Derrick and the fun she could have with him. She quickly made up her mind and told Jessica she would be there.

"You won't regret it, honey, trust me. We are going to have fun," she said while she started twerking.

"I'm not doing all that," Brandy replied as she watched Jessica dance.

The night was young, the drinks were rolling in, and the DJ played all the right music. Brandy hadn't been out since her graduation night. She was really feeling herself, and nothing could ruin her night. She sipped some Hennessy and let the liquor take away all her problems. Clappa and anything else that was negative. While she had Jessica danced to every song, Brandy had her pair of eyes watching her seductive moves. Brandy was prey, and her predator was on the prowl. When the music slowed up, she headed to the bar to order another shot.

"I didn't know you could dance like that," a strong voice said as he took the seat next to Brandy.

"I'm from south-central LA! We get down over there."

"South Central, huh?"

"It's a real long story."

"Ok, so let's leave it at that. What you made you come out tonight?"

"I needed to relieve some stress."

"A pretty woman like you shouldn't be stressing," Derrick said.

Derrick and Brandy sat at the bar conversating and laughing over drinks. It had been a while since Brandy was able to let loose, and really let lose tonight. Her mind was far off Clappa, and she wanted to enjoy herself without the stress.

The more shots she took, the more comfortable she got with Derrick. After a while, nobody else mattered. Her mind was on having a good time, and that's exactly what she did. The next morning Brandy's phone was ringing non-stop, but her massive hangover wouldn't allow her to answer. She tossed and turned while her phone continued to ring. She was sleeping well and didn't want any interruptions. She rolled over to look at the clock sitting on the nightstand and saw it was in the afternoon, so she quickly jumped up. She grabbed her phone and saw she had twelve missed calls from an unknown number.

"Come back to bed, baby, it's early," Derrick said from under the blankets.

Derrick's voice startled Brandy, and she pulled the blankets back to see a half-naked Derrick. The sight of him made her heart skip a beat. She sat at the edge of the bed trying to remember last night's episodes. She let out a deep sigh, and her phone began to ring again. She knew it was Clappa calling, but her guilt wouldn't let her answer, so she stared at the phone until it stopped ringing. Derrick came from behind and started messaging her shoulders while kissing on her neck.

"Don't worry, baby. He'll be just fine. You're with me now. There's no need to stress over dude who's never coming home."

Derrick's words were making Brandy feel more comfortable about the situation, and she started relaxing. Derrick's words were manipulating her thoughts, and she fell for his trap.

"You ready for round two?' asked Derrick.

Brandy didn't say a word. Instead, she stared at him with lust in her eyes, and within seconds round two of last night's adventures begin.

CHAPTER NINE

Six months passed, and Clappa was finally out of the box. He got transferred to U.S.P Hazelton in West Virginia. It was closer to Brandy, but she didn't want anything to do with him. She let Derrick poison her mind with all kinds of negativity about how Clappa wasn't a real man for leaving her behind, and she should move on with her life. The past six months in the box had been up and down for Clappa. The last letter he received from Brandy wasn't good. It seemed like a woman always wants to leave a man when he's doing bad. The upside of Clappa being in the box was he finally got a few letters from pen-pals on I'mTrending. com.

Dear Clappa, 12-07-2007

Hey, Clappa, sorry I haven't been answering your calls or

replying to your letters. Lately, I've been going through many things. I tried to be strong for you. I've been with you since high school, riding and staying by your side, and I loved every minute and second of it. We share so many memories, and for that, I will never forget you and will always have a place in my heart. Unfortunately, I'm afraid this ride ran out of gas, and it's over. I have to move on. I can't pretend like I'm happy anymore. All I do is sit around and wait for that call from jail, and they're telling me you got killed, and my heart can't take it anymore. I hate that it has to come to this, but I have to do things that are best for me and my future. I wish things would have worked out differently for us, but you always wanted to be in the streets. I found a man who loves me for me, and things have been going well for us. I hope you understand and you are happy for me. I will always love you but try to focus on getting some time knocked off. Love always, Brandy.

That letter hit Clappa like a ton of bricks. He never thought Brandy would leave him hanging.

"Damn, Banga was right," he thought as he balled up the letter.

Clappa wasn't too mad, because the letters from I'mTrending.com were flowing in. He couldn't wait to get his property. Once it arrived, he went straight for the pen-pal letters sorting them out and examining every photo. He had over ten letters from all over the world, but one letter and the photo caught his eye.

Dear Antwan, 2-25-08

Hey Antwan, how is everything going? I'm kind of new to this, so sorry if I'm a little plain, lol. I saw your profile on I'mTrending.com and was immediately attracted to you. The look in your eyes was trying to tell me something, so I decided to write you and find out what it was. That might sound kind of lame, but it's the truth.

My name is Charmaine. I'm 25 years old. I'm majoring in business management. I have no kids but plan on having some one of these days, just no time soon. I enjoy reading and walking my dog. I'm kind of a homebody, and I don't go out much. I guess you can say I'm lame, lol. I know what it's like for a person in prison. I have a brother who's been locked up for the past eight years, and that's why I've decided to find someone in prison because everybody needs a friend or a potential lover. I hope you enjoy my pictures and I hope to hear from you soon. Your new friend, Charmaine

Clappa had on an ear-to-ear smile as he read Charmaine's letter. He couldn't believe that with all the time he has to serve, women still want to talk to him. His confidence was slowly growing, and he began to think that he didn't need Brandy. He went through the rest of his letters, then decided to go to the law library, where he met up with an older guy helping him with his law work.

"What are you so jolly about, blood?"

"I got my property today and went through some letters that got from a pen-pal site."

"You need to focus on this law work and not some

female. A pen-pal can't get you out of prison," he said as he pushed a law book in his face.

"Maybe she can help pay for my lawyer fees," replied Clappa.

"Or, maybe she just wants to distract you from the real goal."

"Damn, old head, why are you so grumpy?"

"I've been in jail for the past twenty years helping guys like you get time back or immediate release, and all ya ever think about is some broad," he said as he packed up his books. "Come find me when your mind is on freedom."

Over the next two months, Charmaine and Clappa had been exchanging letters. They talked on the phone every day when she got off work. Clappa had been telling her his problems and agreed to help him with his lawyer fees. She was head over heels for Clappa and wanted more than just letters and phone conversations, so she decided to come see him. Her heart rate increased as she anxiously waited for them to call her name so she could enter the visiting room. Clappa, on the other hand, was in his cell making sure everything was perfect. He brushed and flossed his teeth, he brushed, and he brushed his hair for thirty minutes, then laid it down with a durag.

Seeing Charmaine for the first time in person had Clappa a little nervous. His palms were sweaty, and he barely made eye contact. Once he noticed she had a good sense of humor, he began to loosen up, and the real Clappa come out. They laughed and joked and they talked about their dark pasts. He even told her about Brandy and how hurt he was.

"It's like God sent you to me for a reason," Clappa said as he placed his hand on top of Charmaine's.

She could feel his energy, and she instantly fell in love. When she starred into Clappa's eyes, she could see a future with him, and she had planned on making it work.

"You have five minutes, and visits are over," the guard yelled.

Charmaine's eyes begin to water. She was having such a good time that the thought of leaving Clappa, and Charmaine said their goodbyes and parted ways. The feeling they both felt was unexplainable, but they knew that they wanted more of each other. Charmaine already made a mental note to visit Clappa every weekend until he was released.

Several weeks passed and no visit from Charmaine because the jail was on lockdown. Charmaine made sure to send letters and cards just to show him that he was on her mind. She even sent him some money when she got paid. Charmaine was in love, and she knew it. All she wanted was for Clappa to come home so they could start their life together.

Dear Antwan, 3-30-08

Hey baby, I sent you some cards. I hope when you get them, they put a smile on your face. I'm still mad that I only got to see you once, and the jail went on lockdown. You need to make your way to an FCI ASAP, so we don't have to go through that again. I also sent some money, so make sure you call me as soon as they open the jail back up, and I will make sure I'm there the first week for visits. I hope you like the pics. I took them especially for you. Anyway, baby, stay strong. Love always, Charmaine.

The next day was visit day and Clappa couldn't wait to see his girl. He prepared himself as usual while she stayed in the visiting room. The visit was nice and smooth and feelings between the two were growing, and they were growing fast. Charmaine showed Clappa's lawyers' fees. He was feeling good about his case because he was finally back in court. After meeting Charmaine, he took his legal work more seriously, and during lockdowns, he would study and fish to the old man for insight on the next step he should take.

Being that he was back in court, there was a good chance that he might be going home or getting some time back. He got a letter to China and told her about the good news. He wanted everybody to know that he was on the verge of coming home soon. The good news woke up some unwanted visitors.

Dear Clappa, 5-15-08

Hey, love, how is everything going? I hope by the time you get this letter you will be in the healthiest shape and spirits. First, I want to congratulate you on your success in getting back in court and standing strong. I always knew things would work back in court and standing strong. I can honestly say I'm more than proud that you didn't give up. I know your address. Well, you can thank China for that. I want to apologize for letting you down when you needed me the most. I hope and pray that you can forgive me, and if you can't, it's understood. I just want you to know that you will always have a place in my heart.

Love always, Brandy

Clappa had mixed emotions after reading Brandy's letter. He couldn't understand why she came back. The other side of him was more than happy to hear from her. Brandy was his first love, and nobody can get over their first love, no matter how over and over again, until he came up with a plan on what he should do. His feelings for Charmaine strong, but nothing could replace the good and bad memories that Clappa and Brandy made.

He wanted both of them on the team, being that they were both star players. Before Charmaine came along, it was Brandy that did everything. Clappa wanted Brandy to feel guilty for leaving him for the dead, and he knew just how to do it. He knew he could juggle both women without them ever finding out about each other. He put on a slight grin as his plan came together. His heart was with Charmaine, but he knew Brandy could be beneficial, especially if she knew he had a good chance of coming home.

Clappa sat on his bunk as he let his thoughts and his pen do the rest of the work. He had Brandy right where he wanted her, and there was no turning back. Everything was about to start rolling into place, he thought. A knock at the cell door interrupted Clappa's train of thought, and in came his old lawyer friend.

"I heard about the good news. So, how you feeling, young loc?"

"I feel good, man. I don't think I've ever been happier in life. I want to thank you for everything, OG."

"Yeah, yeah, thank me once you hit those streets. There are a few things I need you to handle when you get out there."

"Don't even trip O.G. I got you," Clappa assured him."

"That's what they all say. Don't be like the rest of these cats, and get to the streets and forget about the good men on the inside. I've helped many of you young cats out, and ya always seem to forget about me. Remember, loyalty is everything, and all you have is your word."

"I'm cut from a different cloth, O.G. I'm not like the rest of the cats."

CHAPTER TEN

The past year had been going well for Clappa. The courts had been giving him nothing but good news, and everything was working for the better after accepting Clappa's 2255 for ineffective assistance of counsel. He instantly filed for an appeal, and things were looking good. Also, Brandy was back in the picture. She could only come once a month for a visit, which made it easy for him to give Charmaine an excuse on why she couldn't come that week. When the jail was on lockdown, it made it even easier for Clappa to come up with lies.

Charmaine dished out a lot of money for lawyer fees. She made it known that she would go the extra mile to get her man out of prison. On the other hand, Brandy was trying to make up for lost time and prove she would never leave him again. Clappa had many questions, like who had she been with, what she had been doing, but he never asked because he didn't want to start a fight, so he just rolled with the punches.

"What are you so happy about?" Brandy asked as Clappa took a seat in the visiting room.

"A lot of reasons. I'm happy to see you, happy about my appeal. I'm just a happy dude right now. Even though I'm still locked up, I feel like nothing can bring me down. Even if I don't win my appeal, I'm still happy that I have you."

"Aww, I love you, baby," she said, and went in for a kiss. "But don't think like that. You should always think you're going to win your appeal. When you come home, I'm going to give you those kids you wanted."

Clappa's face lit up when he heard those words. He always wanted Brandy to be the mother of his kids, but aside from that, he hadn't forgiven her one hundred percent yet. He needed loyalty in a situation that he was in, and Brandy proved she wasn't loyal.

Time was ticking, and Clappa needed to make up his mind on what he was going to do. He had never had so much stress on his plate before, and it was starting to take a toll on him. He hadn't shaved or groomed himself in weeks. He was going back to the free world, and he needed a solid plan. After almost losing his life in the federal system, he didn't want to go out there and do anything stupid that would land him back in prison.

He laid on his back and weighed out his options, and neither one outweighed the other one. He still had unfinished business in Florida, so going back there with Brandy wouldn't be a bad idea, but he had strong feelings for Charmaine, and starting a new life with her wouldn't be so bad either. Clappa's head began to hurt from thinking so much, so he turned his radio and drowned out his thoughts.

Time flew by, and before you knew it, it was time for the 4 o'clock count. Clappa laid on his bed and tried to go to sleep, but thoughts of his best friend Black kept popping up in his head, so he decided to do some push-ups and clear the images out of his head. After the 4 pm court, the CO's ran mail call and, thanks to I'mTrending.com, Clappa had a stack of mail all from new potential pen-pals.

"Damn, they love the kid out there," he said as he walked back to his cell.

"Knock, knock, and knock."

Clappa stopped reading his mail to see that Caine was at his cell door. Caine was a young kid from Compton with two life sentences. He looked at Clappa like an older brother and admired everything about him. Clappa made Caine promises that he would help him out once he hit the streets.

"Damn cuzz, put a nigga on," Caine said while

pointing to the stack of mail.

It's funny how life works out, Clappa thought as he smiled at Caine. He remembered when he just came into the system, and he saw Banga with all the mail. Now it's time to put somebody else on.

Clappa and Caine sat in the cell talking about I'mTrending.com until they called chow. Caine was more than excited to join, but he lacked the funds to do so. Clappa was going to surprise him, and Charmaine set up an account for him. The two laughed and joked about all the females on that site.

Back in the unit, Clappa went straight to work and started replying to all his letters. Even though he had Brandy and Charmaine on his team, he still entertained other women. After Brandy broke bad on him, he would never subject himself to one woman again. He refused to get his heart broken again by women, so he figured why not have a bunch of women.

Weeks and eventually months rolled by. Things with Brandy and Charmaine were going well. Now it was time to get released. Clappa won his appeal and got an immediate release. He couldn't believe this day really came. All the hard work he and the old man put in really paid off. While he was in his cell giving most of his belongings away, his old lawyer friend sat there and gave him simple instructions on what he wanted and needed him to do. Caine sat there excited that Clappa was going home, but he was also sad that his best friend was leaving.

"Let's go, Mr. Jackson, you need to hurry up," the CO said.

Clappa said his final goodbyes as he walked out of the unit. While in R&D, he got to make one phone call, and then he had to head out the door. He had a sweatsuit on and a big photo album, the rest of his possessions he left behind. He walked down to the nearest gas station, which was two miles down the road. He entered the store and asked to use the phone. He tried dialing the number, but it went to voicemail. He tried several more times only to end up with the same results.

"I knew I shouldn't have trusted that bitch!" he screamed, then slammed the phone and walked out of the store.

He looked to his left and then to his right and realized he was in the middle of nowhere. He sat on the bench and felt defeat. He pulled out the $600 check from his pocket that his facility cut for him from the money on his account. He went back inside the gas station, and they immediately shut down all hopes when they told him they don't cash checks.

He walked back outside to get his thoughts together. He put his head in his lap and tried to fight back the tears. He heard tires slowly pull up in front of him, but he paid it no mind.

"So, you just going to sit there with your head down?"

Clappa slowly raised his head to see an all-black 750 series BMW and the driver was Charmaine. A smile instantly spread across his face, and he jumped up in excitement.

"Damn, baby, you had me stressed. I thought you wasn't coming," Clappa said as he entered the car.

"Why would you think that? Once you called me this morning and told me you got released, I jumped in my car. I got you, baby. You don't ever have to worry about me doing you wrong."

Clappa smiled and gave Charmaine a big kiss, and then the two drove off to start their new life.

Freedom

From the Cage to L.A.

Clappa hopped in the 750 BMW. Once his back touched the luxury seats, he was at ease.

"Baby, I thought you got lost or forgot about your man."

"Seriously? How could I lose any thoughts revolving around your fine self?"

"Sweetheart, you looking better than Rihanna. Let's go to a telly so I can hit you in a sauna (laughs)."

"Little do you know I already have a hotel reserved at the Howard Johnson. Baby, I got you a new outfit and an iPhone 12 waiting at the room. Oh, I almost forgot, here. She handed Clappa a stack of hundred-dollar bills that were long ways with a seal going around them. "Ten biscuits."

"C'mon bae, you ain't have to give me all this money."

"I'll give you whatever I wanna give you."

"That's a lot of dough, let me find out you slanging and banging on the shawty 10 (laughs)."

"Clappa, you is crazy. I'm glad to see you got your sense of humor."

They finally made it to the hotel room. The full-size suite was dark, with candles lit. Vanilla frosting aroma filled the room. A bottle of Jenny Down Cellars Rose Wine sat next to the warm sauna.

"You got this joint laid out like this for me, bae?"

"You're dealing with a very romantic woman, remember that."

Clappa couldn't refrain any longer. He pulled his dick out of his pants. (Deep breath)

"Oh my goodness, baby, I don't know if I'm ready for all that."

His manhood stood out of tension like a pit bull's tail when he's ready to attack. Clappa wasted no time aggressively ripping off her leggings and muscle brawl.

"Not so fast, baby. Take your time. I haven't been

touched by a man in years. My cat is sensitive."

Clappa picked her up in his arms and carried her to the California king-size bed. Clappa stripped down to nothing but his socks. Their eyes were locked as they kissed passionately. She rolled over on top of Clappa, slowly easing her head low. She licked and kissed all over his sculpted chiseled chest and six-pack.

"Mmmm, hold fast, baby, that's too fast. I ain't tryna let loose."

She ignored Clappa's plea, deep throating and slobbering until his seeds squirted all over her pretty face and soft pink lips.

"You're still standing? Bae, what you tryna do to me?"

"Make you put a ring on it."

She reserved cowgirl on him in a slow rhythm while Ella Mai's Found played softly in the background. Clappa lifted her up then flipped her around a doggy style position. He swiped his tongue up and down her shaved crack like a black card.

"Oh my God Clappa, I'm gonna have your babies."

She turned her over on her clit. Within 60 seconds, her legs started to tremble. She moaned and screamed while experiencing her climax.

"Put it in, put it in."

Clappa slid in her, nearly getting jammed up. He wasn't even halfway inside before he came.

"Baby, type Missy Elliot's Minute Man song on

YouTube.”

"You got be bent cuzz?”

"Shut up,” she told Clappa as she threw a friendly jab.

"Ok beautiful, I see you on your MMA stuff, tuff.”

They laid on each other naked for about thirty minutes.

"Baby, let me show you your outfit.”

She pulled out the Gucci bag and handled it to Clappa. There was an all-white Gucci belt with chrome double G's on the buckle, an all-white Gucci button-up, and some white silk Gucci slacks. "Thank you, bae.”

"Here baby, here's your iPhone 12. It's already activated through T-Mobile with a full ninety-day activation, unlimited talk, text, web, etc. You can drive the Beemer until you get some wheels. I'll just use my dad's 2020 Silverado black ops pickup truck.”

"Dang, baby, you can control that big boy truck?”

"You know first-hand that I know how to control big things.”

"Yeah, alright.”

"So, are you going to move in with me?”

"Where else you think Imma go? I'm definitely not going back to the jets.”

"I was just asking a question, smarty.”

"The high-rise downtown L.A. where we stay is cool baby, do you think your PO gonna trip?”

"Nah, it'll be straight.”

"Some dude been hitting your IG and Facebook page. You know him?"

"Ain't no question; that's my homie Reaper that just got back off a double."

"Bae, please don't get caught back in conspiracy or something worse."

"I feel you, baby, but I'll never let my real ones see the name on the back of my jersey, meaning I won't turn my back."

Clappa poured a cup of wine and put on his baby powder white Versace robe to step on the hotel balcony. He dialed up Reaper's number. The phone rang twice before Reaper picked up.

"Who this is, cuzz?"

"This Clappa cuzz, I'm out the federal cage back in LA."

"Where you at solider?"

"At the telly with my main squeeze"

"Fasho had to pull ya stick out the mud."

"Ain't no, secret cuzz."

"Can you pull up on me, or baby girl got you miracle whipped already?"

"C'mon cuzz, you know I'mma player."

"Give me about thirty-five minutes, and I'mma pull up."

"Where you posted at?"

"38th and Western, it's a 2019 Mercedes Benz Amg

GT 63, sitting in front of a white house."

"What color is the Benz cuzz?"

"Royal blue with tints on it."

"You still banging hard, Reaper."

"Ima thug it out until that wooden frame drop."

"Baby, who you talking to?"

"My homie reaper. Listen sweetheart, I went through enough interrogation with the feds."

"If you say you my man, I got the right to ask you whatever I want."

"Just chill, baby. I'm only interested in you. I need to go slide on my homie Reaper, so he can lace my Gucci shoes."

"What does that mean?"

"Bring me up to speed on what been going on in the hood."

"Why you even worried about that?"

"Look, baby girl, I refuse to let somebody put me on a designer shirt. I never been the victim from the streets to the pen"

"Alright, bae, just be careful. I'll meet you at the high rise late on tonight."

"You need me to drop you off?"

"No, bae, my dad is gonna pick me up so I can have dinner with him and my mom."

"Give me a kiss."

"Be safe, Clappa"

"My middle name is safety."

Clappa crept slowly in the white Beemer banging Nipsey Hussle blue laces. The hood was different than when he left 12 years ago. He pulled over behind the royal blue Benz in front of the white house. Reaper came through the side of the house and jumped in the passenger seat.

"Give me some love, cuzz."

"I ain't with all that hugging, Clappa,"

"You still ol tuff Reaper."

"Man cuzz, I'm out here warring just cause, them people overturned them doubles don't mean the streets overturned it. You see my youngins in the cut with them K's. They gone eject the whole hundred at my command."

"How we gone get money and war at the same time, Reaper?"

"I'll figure out away."

"It ain't no way, homie. Remember Crypto cuzz"

"Yeah, that's my homie."

"He got shipped from new Folsom prison to pelican bay."

"What cuzz in there doing?"

"You already know playing with the knife. He got his appeal; in six months, he'll be home."

"I need cuzz info so I can drop this five G's on his account."

Clappa pulled out his bankroll and counted five bands.

"You fresh out the pen cuzz, you really finna drop all that cash on cuzz books?"

"Me and Crypto was fifty-fifty relationship. Me and cuzz would split a nutty bar together, this money ain't nothing."

"I respect that cuzz."

"Reaper, make sure that you give cuzz my number as soon as he hit yo line. Take this bread if you could cuzz go to the Western Union for me. I gotta make it to the spot before my PO show up tonight."

"I got you cuzz."

"Alright, Reaper be smooth."

Clappa headed to the high rise earlier than Charmaine expected.

"Hey, baby girl, I'm home. I thought you was going out to eat with your parents?"

"I had to reschedule due to your probation officer calling me."

"What he say?"

"He was on his way just to look at the place. You hear that bae? That's the PO."

"Charmaine, let me do the talking, ok?"

"I'm not gonna get involved in y'all convo, bae."

"How you doing there, sir?"

"Hey Clappa."

Clappa's eyes got big in disbelief of his PO calling him by his nickname.

"Ima cut straight through straight through the surface. You're a dangerous guy Clappa. I seen everything you been suspected of in your career in the streets of L.A."

"No sir, that's not, with all due respect," Clappa shut up.

"I'm laying down the law here. I'll see to it that you're back shackled up on an airplane. You're not to be around other gang members, or no dirty UAs, and if you're around any firearms, you'll be charged under the U.S. Code ACCA, armed 924(e) Career Criminal Act. Well, Clappa, just take a mental note of everything I said. I'll be back in a month."

"Yeah, whatever, cuzz."

Clappa's PO was on him. One slip and fall is all it may take for Clappa never to get up again.

"Tonight is Friday, Bae, do you wanna go out to the club Nuevo in Beverly Hills?"

"I don't know, baby."

"Clappa, why you acting stubborn, your PO left so you're free to have fun."

"You right, baby girl, gone get yourself together, so we can go out."

10 minutes later, Charmaine walked out the bathroom in a dark Vader, black Chanel skirt, with some red bottom hills. Her red black Chanel frames matched

perfectly with her outfit.

"Baby, you're red-carpet Oscar material, boy I tell ya."

Clappa was speechless. He didn't know whether to take her out or to get back in her guts. The club was cracking. Clappa walked in the Club Nuevo with Charmaine's arm wrapped around his.

"Sit your beautiful self down at the bar while I go to the restroom, baby."

Clappa took a piss then washed his hands.

"Where you from?"

"South central LA."

"I'm from Atlanta, GA, but my uncle OG blue from watts."

"OK, they call me Clappa."

"I'm C-fly."

"You bang C-fly?"

"I'm cripping these millions I'm flipping. I just signed a multi-million-dollar deal with cutthroat records."

"Yea cuzz, I'm familiar with cutthroat records."

"What table you at Clappa?"

"I'm right there posted where that fine dime sitting."

"Ima send two bottles of Ace of Spades, one for you and your gorgeous lady."

"Good looking C-fly."

"That ain't nothing, me and my unk blow at least thirty G's every Friday night."

"Baby girl, I want you to meet somebody."

"That's C-fly."

"You know him?"

"Who don't know him? His album made number one on Billboard charts."

"There go my Unk OG Blue over there with that black and white tux on."

"Let's go over there so you can meet him."

"Unk this Clapp from South Central, LA."

"You just got out the feds youngster?"

"Yeah"

"So I finally get to meet you, Clappa, I know your G homies."

"C-fly, this dude is a trained assassin. We gone get him out them streets, and put him under our umbrella, so the rain don't hit him."

They spent the rest of the night parlaying. Charmaine and Clappa woke up the next morning in Fendi silk sheets.

"Clappa, I feel like I got a hangover, baby."

"Don't trip, baby girl, Ima go get you some headache medicine out the bathroom."

Clappa walked to the bathroom in his slippers and Polo briefs.

"Here, baby, this 800 mg."

"Thank you, bae."

Clappa's phone rings.

"What's cracking"

"You have a collect call from an inmate at California Pelican Bay prison. Do you accept the call?"

"Yeah, I accept."

"What's cracking cuzz?"

"Clappa, you knew I'm flagging in these trenches."

"When you get out, cuzz?"

"Yesterday. Man, cuzz, I looked on my account and seen 5 G's Reaper sent that on behalf. Good looking cuzz. I see breaking bread in yo direction."

"The only way I switch is if I'm hitting them on a drop. Six more months' cuzz and these devils gotta let me go."

"Yeah, Reaper told me cuzz."

"You better have me something clean waiting on me to hop in."

"Let me get my weight up first."

"The phone finna go out cuzz."

"Already cuzz."

Charmaine cooked breakfast for Clappa before he left the crib. Phone rings.

"Clappa, this OG blue. Me and C-fly wanted to know if you could come out here to LA Habra Heights, California."

"I'm in rue right now OG."

"Ok cuzz, the address is 740 Church Hill."

"What ya'll in a mansion cuzz?"

"That's how we living, youngsta."

Clappa pulled in the driveway of the 4,076 square feet mansion. Two 2019 Rolls Royce Cullinan's sat in the driveway. One was a two-tone white and Orlando Magic blue. The second one was a strawberry Now and Later red.

OG Blue came to the expensive glass door.

"You made it quick, youngsta."

"What up, cuzz?"

"C-fly what it do cuzz?"

"Bout to go to Henson's recording studio in L.A."

"You gone stay here with me, Clappa, so we can build cuzz. This lil model chick on her way to scoop me, I'm not taking the double R"

"You gotta get the strap and tuck it C"

"I got it unk."

"A youngsta, this is how you'll live if you join the winning team. Four bedrooms, four full bathrooms, upstairs master suite with a private balcony, jacuzzi, fireplace, golf course, with full-court customized basketball court."

"No disrespect OG, but this stuff don't excite me at all. If I got to get out the slums I will. One thing OG my p's don't bend lawn chairs do."

"Man, youngsta, you remind me of your homie, rest his soul. I would never put you in a situation to where you have to bend what you stand on. You a hitter, youngsta, and I know who taught you the war tactics you possess. Basically, we need you to be our top security dude. We is giving you a cool breeze quarter Milly, with any automobile you want."

"So, what shifts ya'll tryna have me when we hit Hollywood, and Vegas."

Clappa and OG blue shook hands like two mob bosses. OG Blue reached in the closet and handed Clappa a night hawk superb quality 45 with a red dot sight system on it.

"Be careful youngsta, it's fully loaded to the capacity."

"So, what we gone go to 310 Motors for the wheels?"

"Youngsta, we order from DuPont registries. Look in this exotic car buyers guide."

OG Blue hands Clappa the magazine.

"I want this 2019 Lamborghini Urus, $237,951 is the price tag. All you gotta do is tell me what color and the address you want it shipped to."

"Everything royal blue OG. Have it shipped to the downtown high rise in L.A. down the street from the Staples Center."

"I forgot one thing."

OG blue Clappa grabbed a cream and white color Louis Vuitton duffle bag from the back of the two-tone white and blue Cullinan.

"That's all honchos youngsta consider the deal complete."

Two Weeks Later

Clappa sat in his Lamborghini Urus seat leaned back, smoking a blunt filled with OG. He watched the L.A news on his 8 1/2-inch monitor when breaking news hit.

"There was an older black man who was murdered in this Mercedes Benz earlier this morning. He was slain execution-style by two suspects who fled the scene with fully equipped assault rifles. Here is a picture of the victim."

When Clappa seen Reaper's face, he dropped the blunt on the floorboard.

"Cuzz, nah, they done smoked the homie," he said outloud.

Clappa sat there for another hour in disbelief. Later on that night, he, C-fly, and OG Blue went to Vegas Sin City. They bought thousands of dollars' worth of gambling chips and shot dice. Clappa couldn't focus. He went in the parking lot back-to-back, smoking loud blunts. Clappa never told OG Blue or C-fly about the fallen soldier. Clappa never exposed his personal business. Within the next few months, Clappa's drug habit got worse and more expensive.

One day Clappa was scrolling through his inbox on Facebook, when his old lover Brandy popped up.

"If you're reading this message, call this number A.S.A.P"

Phone rings.

"Hello, this Brandy?"

"This is her,"

"This is Clappa, boo."

"So Clappa, you gone get out and move on without even reaching out back for me?"

"Hey, sometimes life takes twists and turns you can't control."

"Then China talking about y'all about to get married."

"Shorty lying. I ain't seen her since I been out the feds. Brandy I don't got time for this right now. I'm still tryna get over Reaper getting drowned."

"Yeah, I heard about it. Sorry to hear that. Just call me when you're not busy Clappa."

"I got you cuzz."

"Bye Clappa."

Right when Clappa thought it couldn't get any worse, he was wrong.

Club Night

"C-fly, who is cuzz OG blue arguing with?"

"I don't know, but if he keeps moving his hands like that, we gone bust em."

The night passed quickly, and there were so many pretty women, liquor, kush, and disco lights. When Clappa, C-fly and, OG blue walked out of the club, choppa gunfire erupted in the parking lot. OG Blue was hit in the face and torso. Clappa upped his 45 hid behind the double R truck and started busting back at the three gunmen. These hitters were trained and had to have premeditated this hit.

They all wore one-piece cart hart black suits, ski mask, black gloves, and black shoes. It was like black apes with AK 47's. C-fly got hit in the back of his head in the process of trying to run behind the truck where Clappa was. Once the gunfire smoke cleared, Clappa ran to check on OG Blue and C-fly. OG Blue was soulless right there on the spot.

"C-fly, wake up," Clappa said as he held him in his arms.

As bad as Clappa wanted to stay there with C-Fly, he knew his PO would violate him quick. Clappa jumped in his Lambo truck and left rubber marks behind due to how fast he peeled out.

Five Months Later

OG Blue was in a wooden framework six feet beneath, and C-fly was a vegetable. The only good thing Clappa had going was his main man's Crypto been home with him getting things in order. Clappa was almost broke and lost Charmaine. He was on and off dealing with a chick out of Berkeley, California. She was a college girl that had no idea what Clappa was into. They had what you call a distant lover relationship.

The only thing that kept Clappa afloat is Crypto gave him fifty grand when he touched. Clappa went from a Lam truck, a cool quarter million, a woman who had a high rise and a Beemer, to living in the same area. Reaper got murdered and driving a Plain-Jane Honda Civic.

"Yo Clappa, you never gone believe this cuzz."

"What up cuzz?"

"I heard through one of the kush plugs I got that OG Blue and C-fly got hit up cause they ran off with a hundred kilos of heroin from the Columbians."

"C-fly probably didn't know what was going on with OG blue C-fly was a multi-millionaire, you really think he was straddling the fence?"

"You know how greed makes dudes think. We need a hustle Crypto."

"I told you cuzz, I got a few kush plugs."

"How much paper you got left from that fifty Clappa?"

"Bout thirty"

"You need to chill on the drugs, cuzz."

"Give me twenty G's and put ten in the cat somewhere."

Clappa gave Crypto the twenty grand so he could double up. Crypto never took Clappa with him to the plug's crib in the bay Seminary Street in Oakland, California, was a gold mine with different exotic kush from cookie, blue dream, OG, and more. Down 38th and Western, Crypto slid in his raiders grey and black Regal with gold Daytons on it.

"Clappa, who is this?"

"This is Lil D.E."

"D.E, yeah, that' what they call me."

"How you get that nickname?"

"I caught my first 187 with a D.E. I put the desert eagle to his face and watched his face erase."

"Clappa, let me holla at you cuzz."

"Why you bring this lil wild boy over here?"

"We can have him run kush spot."

"He's a killer and a hustler. Crypto, that's the type of lil homie we need around."

"Cool, I'm letting you know Clappa, first time he do something dealing with our cash, you gone smoke em."

"He good cuzz. Just back in the Regal and stack these pringles."

In the next few weeks, Lil D.E was doing football numbers on the weed. Crypto was surprised how strong Lil cuzz hustle was. Clappa was in a 2019 G wagon Benz in no time and Crypto upgraded to a 2019 Jag.

Knock, Knock it's the FEDS.

Lil D.E. was in big trouble. The Feds kicked in the door with machine guns drawn. They found like a hundred and seventy pounds of grade a kush and two hundred thousand in cash. They tore up the living room wall and found two AR 15's with a 380 Jennings handgun. Come to find out, Lil D.E. had a triple homicide pending which was why the Feds even hit the spot. Lil D.E. was read his rights and booked into the L.A. County Jail. Crypto found out about the raid before Clappa did.

Phone rings.

"Clappa, a cuzz clam down Crypto. I told you about Lil D.E."

"What happened, cuzz?"

"He got the spot ransacked by the feds. They took everything cuzz."

"Lil cuzz was wanted for a triple homicide. This falls on you, Clappa. Now we gotta worry about him pulling a first 48 break."

"Chill cuzz, you know baby girl Tasha out of Berkeley Collage is a paralegal. The lawyer that she works under is one of the best in the whole state of California. Ima have them look into his whole situation to make sure he got gorilla glue on his lips."

Clappa got up with Tasha and broke the whole situation down. She investigated everything. Lil D.E was solid as of right now.

Back On 38th & Western

"That's too much cash to be tryna count,"

"I got the money machine in the G wagon."

"What you waiting on, Clappa, hurry and go get it cuzz."

They were putting money in that machine for at least one hour. When the count was complete, they were sitting on 1.7 million.

"Cuzz, we about to shoot to Vegas,"

"Crypto, you tripping Cuzz, we need to get out of the region."

"Where did you have in mind, cuzz?"

Suddenly, bangs were coming from the front and backdoor that sounded like mighty thunder was tryna get in.

"Cuzz get the extra clips."

"Crypto, you think it's the feds?"

"Whoever it is cuzz, we blazing, we ain't doing no hesitating."

Was it the feds coming due to what happened with Lil D.E, or was it the swat team tracking them down for the deadly home invasion? Maybe the Oakland boys followed them looking to retaliate. Whatever the case was, it was about to be closed.

1. Are you team Clappa, team Brandy, or team Charmaine?
2. Do you think Brandy tried to hold him down?
3. Do you think Clappa pushed her away?
4. Do you think Clappa should have got out in still dealt with Brandy?
5. Do you think Charmaine deserved all of Clappa?
6. Would you ever meet someone on a dating site that's incarcerated?
7. What type of bond does Crypto and Clappa have?
8. Do you think anything can come between their bond?
9. What do you think happened to Clappa, Crypto, Brandy, China, Charmaine, and Chiquita, better yet what you want to see happen to them?
10. Would you be able to stay loyal to your man or woman? How and why?

I look forward to your answers and your input. I promise to respond back to all mail. I love snail mail so get at me. Anthony Gardner 29788112 USP Atwater PO Box 019001 Atwater, CA 95301

FEDERAL PUBLIC DEFENDER
CENTRAL DISTRICT OF CALIFORNIA
321 EAST 2nd STREET
LOS ANGELES, CALIFORNIA 90012-4202
213-894-2854
213-894-0081 FAX

AMY M. KARLIN
Interim Federal Public Defender
CUAUHTEMOC ORTEGA
Chief Deputy

AMY M. KARLIN
Branch Chief
Southern Division
ANGELA VIRAMONTES
Branch Chief
Eastern Division

October 25, 2019

Anthony Gardner | Reg. #29788-112
USP Lee
U.S. Penitentiary
P.O. Box 305
Jonesville, VA 24263

Re: <u>**USA v. Anthony Gardner, CA9 17-56160 (*Johnson* appeal)**</u>

Dear Mr. Gardner:

I received your letter dated October 17, 2019. I know waiting must be frustrating, but your case is still stayed pending *Begay* and *Dominguez* -- both of which are technically still pending. An opinion was filed in *Begay*, but the government is asking for the court to reconsider that decision and they are filing a brief next month. *Dominguez* is set for oral argument in December - after oral argument, the same thing that happened in *Begay* will happen in that case (a petition for panel rehearing after the decision comes out) no matter the outcome.

I am printing you a docket for each case: *Begay*, *Dominguez*, and your own *Johnson* appeal and enclosing the *Begay* opinion. If you have additional questions about your case, please call Ms. Mitchell, you can always call us collect at (213) 894-2854.

Thank you for the well-wishes and keeping in contact. I will certainly let you know when there is movement in your appeal.

ABOUT THE AUTHOR

Anthony Gardner was born and raised in Los Angeles, CA. Always was a wild always was a wild child who eventually turned into a wild man. Like every other black man with no guidance but the streets and gangs, he landed in prison serving 389 months. Mr. Gardner has been in federal prison since 2004. He has accomplished his brand. "I'm Trending," he has studied and received his G.E.D., but most of all, he has different respect, value, and outlook on life. His motto is "the sky is the limit," and he won't be stopped.

To contact Mr. Gardner AKA sponge look him up on FBOP.gov or write Anthony Gardner 29788112 USP Atwater Po Box 019001 Atwater, CA 95301

Edward Coleman, we walked it down period and stood tall. How everyone else free. We on our way, the Appeal should be ruled soon… Appeal on the way I will be free soon; look out!

www.ingramcontent.com/pod-product-compliance
Lightning Source LLC
Chambersburg PA
CBHW060556100726
47907CB00005B/1381